HOOAH

A story of improbable relationships in the inferno of war

Dan Daniels

HOOAH: An affirmative exclamation used by soldiers of the US military that harken back to the Revolutionary War. "Heard, Understood, Acknowledged" (HUA). An expression of enthusiasm, motivation, and a can-do attitude. More than just a word, it's a mindset that soldiers have, enabling them to push through difficult times and accomplish the mission, no matter what obstacle they may face.

combat boot prints in the hourglass sand of time, and the wind thereafter leaving no trace, yet that interlude in life will live forever in the heart of those who walked in the shadow of death

CHAPTER I

sniper training

After basic training, Taylor requested to go to ranger school and was accepted into the program. After ten weeks of training, he was assigned to the 75th Ranger Regiment.

Having excelled at marksmanship, he was selected for sniper school.

***

It was 02:00 hours on a moonless night when the MH-6 "Little Bird" helicopter landed in a small valley between rolling hills. With the engine still running, the pilot slapped him on the back as Army Specialist Taylor Lawton exited the aircraft. He instinctively bent down as he walked away from the helicopter because the rotor blades felt like they were inches from his head. "I bet the tribe a case of beer that you bang the man, so don't let me down," the pilot said as the helicopter lifted off.

From the hustle of loading and checking his gear to the noise of the chopper fading into the distance, suddenly, it was quiet except for the calming sounds of nature.

Taylor trained for weeks, preparing for this day. But, to become a sniper, he must pass a final test. The rules specified he could only travel during daylight hours. So, he was glad he had the time before daylight to relax and adjust to the environment. He molded his backpack into a pillow and gazed at the stars.

Searching for relevance and contemplating the future, he imagined being a Viking warrior in an alternate life and ultimately standing at the entrance to Valhalla.

He was drinking coffee when the sun slowly illuminated the landscape. He was surrounded by large old-growth trees that created a canopy of foliage so thick that it prevented the sunlight from reaching the ground. Little vegetation was growing on the forest floor because of the constant shade. It made walking easy but also easy to be seen.

The goal of the training exercise that Taylor was about to undertake was to find his way to a location thirty miles away with only a topographic map of the area and a lensatic compass. He had two canteens of water but would have to forage for food as he journeyed to his target while evading simulated enemy soldiers looking for him. If he makes it to his destination without being spotted, there is a roped-off 100 square yards of tall grass and thorny bushes he must enter and crawl until he finds red marking tape on the ground. At that point, he could shoot the metal silhouette of an enemy soldier hanging on a steel rod four hundred yards away. He must hit the bull's eye on the target's chest with a single shot.

During this part of the exercise, two soldiers with binoculars would be standing on a platform about two feet high overlooking the roped-off area, searching for the slightest unnatural movement that would expose his position. If he is spotted before he shoots, he fails the course.

Buddies that had completed the course gave him all the advice they could think of, but the bottom line was, did he have what it takes to overcome any obstacle, be it an insect biting the crap out of you, a tactical error, or a lapse of concentration.

After clearing his mind of everything except the task ahead, he drank water from one of his canteens to hydrate while studying his map and compass. Having established a heading, he shouldered his backpack and started the exercise.

There was an animal trail running in the direction he was heading, but he knew that was not a good choice. The simulating bad guys would probably be watching it.

Progressing through the forest, the landscape changed to scattered bushes and small, gnarly trees in rocky terrain. Traversing the terrain became more difficult, but there were plentiful huckleberry bushes. He gathered a pocket of berries to snack on and saved the rest for dinner.

It was getting late on his first day when he started looking for a campsite. Walking alongside a stream for over an hour, he set up camp on a gravel bar jutting into the stream. After unloading his gear, he gathered a pile of leaves to make a semi-comfortable pad for his sleeping bag. After setting up camp, he turned his attention to food. He had a small fish-casting net that a buddy had given him. After a few tries throwing it, he caught two fish and grilled them over a fire with a stick fashioned into a skewer. He went to sleep with a full stomach.

It was barely daylight when he was awakened by a huffing sound coming from the other side of the stream. Raising himself enough to see across the stream, a grizzly bear was standing on its back legs, looking at him.

As he had been advised to do when confronting a bear, he eased out of his sleeping bag, bolted a round into his rifle, and started talking in a normal tone while moving around the campsite. Taylor had no intention of shooting the bear, but he was ready in case the grizzly was having a bad hair day. He had also been told not to make eye contact but to watch with his peripheral vision. He threw a log on the fire while watching the bear's every move. The bear was so close that if he charged, Taylor would have only a few seconds to shoot.

After about five minutes, which felt like an hour, the grizzly ambled down the bank of the stream away from him.

nothing like having a seven-hundred-pound grizzly bear wake you up to start the day

After a cup of coffee to settle his nerves, he broke camp and headed to a knoll that would give him an unobstructed view of the terrain. He glassed the area with binoculars looking for the bad guys. After a thorough search, he continued to his destination.

On day two, the sun sank below the horizon, and it started raining. He built a simple lean-to shelter with tree limbs and stretched a tarp over it to protect him from the rain.

He ate berries and fish he had saved. He spent the next hour reviewing every detail of how he would attack his target. Finally, confident with his plan, he retired to his sleeping bag to get a good night's rest.

On the final day of the course, Taylor thought he would have encountered the bad guys by now but understood the psychological part of the exercise. Now he didn't know if the bad guys were out there or if the two guys on the platform were the only obstacles in his way.

He had to assume the bad guys were close by, so he planned accordingly. He attached local vegetation to his Ghillie suit and rifle, making him undetectable to the untrained eye. He pulled the bolt back on his sniper rifle to double-check the bullet in the chamber.

He was so determined to pass the test he had decided to crawl the last fifty yds. He figured that should eliminate any possibility of the bad guys spotting him. Then all he had to do was crawl to the firing line tape and shoot the target before the guys spotted him.

He remembered his buddies talking about critters crawling into their clothing. So, he cut lengths of parachute cord to tie his pant legs and shirt sleeves tight against his boots and gloves.

Having crawled halfway to the target, he felt good about his progress until he saw an enemy soldier off to his left, not twenty feet from him. Then another soldier appeared beyond the first soldier. They were combing the tall grass looking for him.

He watched the soldiers search the area before he crawled in behind them, assuming they wouldn't cover the same ground again.

He could see the guys on the platform now. He was only a few yards from the firing line tape. He forced himself to slow down. This was the point where many failed the course because they lost their concentration and got busted.

He was searching for the firing line tape when a rattlesnake slithered across his path. The snake sensed him and coiled up into its striking posture. Taylor eased the barrel of his gun toward it. Flicking its tongue, the snake struck the weapon's muzzle before slinking away.

The barely perceptible sound of the grass swaying in the light wind and the cry of a hawk circling overhead was shattered by the muzzle blast from Taylor's rifle. The bullet slammed into the bull's eye of the target with a violent bang that startled the simulating enemy soldiers even though they were expecting it. Taylor stood up, and the soldiers working the exercise gave him a big "Hooah."

CHAPTER II

first combat

Taylor was assigned to 2nd Platoon, Company B, of the 75th Ranger Regiment, destined for Iraq. He looked out the window of the C-17 as it turned on final approach to Forward Operating Base (FOB) Diamondback.

After two weeks of orientation, his platoon boarded two Blackhawk Helicopters and headed for their first combat patrol. The area they were heading to was purportedly secure and should be an easy break-in patrol for the new "green bean" troops. No contact with the enemy was expected. The landing zone (LZ) was in a valley about a mile long and two hundred yards wide.

Everyone was uptight, not knowing how they would react to combat, even though they expected this to be an easy, uneventful patrol. The Blackhawks touched down, and everyone started exiting with their gear. The helicopters were making so much noise and dust that Taylor could barely hear or see anything. When a buddy fell, Taylor thought he had stumbled, but when he reached down to help him, he saw he had been shot in the neck just above his body armor. Disbelief and shock engulfed him. In combat thirty seconds and a buddy was dead.

He was stunned when a bullet hit his body armor, knocking him to the ground. Looking through the dust and flying debris, he saw a large number of enemy soldiers advancing on his position. A Rocket Propelled Grenade (RPG) hit one of the helicopters as it lifted off and fell back to the ground in a ball of fire. Mortar, machine gun, RPG, and rifle fire came from every direction. They were surrounded and outnumbered. The Radio Telephone Operator (RTO), bleeding from a bullet wound to his arm, was yelling into his handset for air support. The lieutenant lying beside him was dead.

Green troops on their first combat mission were thrust into a firestorm of combat. On pure adrenaline, Taylor picked up a downed soldier's M249 belt-fed machine gun and threw his weapon and two bandoliers of ammo over his shoulder.

Al-Radea fighters were everywhere. On one knee, he started shooting, with rounds from the machine gun ripping the enemy ranks. He spotted a small ravine he could use for protection and ran toward it, firing as he went. Leaping into the ravine, a grenade exploded a few yards away, knocking him to the ground. With adrenaline pumping and numb from the sudden chaos, he jumped to his feet as an enemy soldier lunged at him with a bayoneted rifle. With one motion, he blocked the bayonet with his weapon and fired point-blank into his assailant's chest.

Through the adrenaline, he felt a burning sensation in his left thigh. Glancing down, he saw his pant leg soaked in blood. Fighting with every ounce of willpower to keep from passing out, he took a trauma patch from his backpack and applied it to his leg to stop the bleeding.

Through the haze of smoke and hell, he saw a buddy go down. He made his way to him and, grabbing the collar of his body armor, dragged him out of the line of fire and into the ravine.

He dressed his buddy's wound and pushed him into a small cavity under the roots of a tree created by erosion from water running through the ravine when it rained. "Be quiet, don't move," Taylor said as he threw branches of dead vegetation against the tree roots to better hide him.

The battle continued for another thirty minutes before it suddenly stopped. Time stood still. His mind couldn't comprehend what had happened. The moment was surreal. It was eerily quiet after the firestorm of the previous hour. He strained to see or hear anything that might determine the situation. He saw movement to his right and raised his weapon to fire, expecting an Al-Radea soldier to attack him.

"Taylor?" a muffled voice asked.

He didn't make a sound.

"Taylor, it's Ed."

It's one of his guys.

"Yeah, Ed, can you tell if the Al-Radea soldiers have left?" he whispered.

"I think they have moved back into the mountains," Ed responded.

The dustoffs (medevac helicopters) landed in the same location as the Blackhawks had landed earlier. He held his breath, expecting all hell to break loose again, but there was no firing. The Al-Radea soldiers had vanished into the mountains.

It took several hours for the medics to stabilize the wounded before loading them and the dead into the choppers. Three soldiers died, and five were seriously wounded in the battle.

***

In the air heading back to base, Taylor leaned forward to a buddy lying on the floor of the dustoff with a towel folded under his head. He had blood-soaked bandages around his head and both arms. Taylor lit a cigarette and placed it between his bloody fingers.

There was blood on the floor and everyplace a hand had grabbed onto a part of the chopper.

Sitting in the open doorway of the helicopter as it headed back to base, he watched the ground stream below him as he tried to make sense of what had happened.

He looked at his buddy, Ed, and saw that thousand-yard stare he had only heard about before now, that hollow, blank stare. He touched his arm to get his attention, offered him a cigarette, and took one himself. With a bloody hand, Ed took the cigarette without comment. Taylor took a long drag on his cigarette and gazed out across the desert below him as it faded into the distance. The experience seared into his brain.

***

He was lucky the grenade shrapnel that hit him glanced off the pistol in his leg holster first before the jagged piece gashed his leg. He had lost blood, but nothing major was damaged. He was in the base hospital for a few days before returning to his unit.

The remaining guys of the platoon were now forever bonded in blood. They weren't just members of an infantry unit anymore, they were brothers.

CHAPTER III

Taylor meets future wife

His platoon was so shot up they were ordered to stay at the main base in Mosul until his platoon could be restored to combat-ready status.

One evening he and his buddy Ed went to the USO club to relax and drink a beer. Looking over the room, he noticed the nurse who had tended him in the hospital. She was talking with friends when he approached her. He remembered her name. "Hello, Lee, you probably don't remember me, but you checked on me several times while recuperating from a little wound."

"Giving shots all day, I usually see more butts than faces. So, drop your pants, and I will see if I remember you," she laughed.

"Yes, I remember you Lawton, Taylor Lawton, right?"

"And to speed up the conversation, none of us are looking to get laid tonight, thank you," Lee's friend, Shari, declared.

Relationships in a combat zone took on a unique perspective. You dealt with people as if you may not see them again after that time. "Give me a break. I haven't socialized with an American gal in a while. How about a drink and some down-home conversation?" he asked.

Liz, the third girl in the group, jokingly commented to her friends. "A homesick Joe, he probably hasn't been "in country" a month, but what the heck, you ladies up for it?"

"Sure," said Lee.

"Okay," added Shari.

"Do you mind if my buddy joins us?" Taylor asked, pointing to his friend, Ed.

"Okay, but tell him we just want to enjoy a pleasant evening with some decent guys. We've all had bad experiences and have become pretty wary of you guys."

Taylor went to Ed and asked him if he would like to have a drink with the girls.

"Sounds good, but are you sure you want company?" Ed asked.

"Heck yeah, these gals may abuse me if I'm alone."

After joining the girls, Liz commented she would stay at the club.

"Please, come with us. I don't want y'all to feel paired up with Ed and me. Let's just hang out and enjoy the evening. How about something to eat? Have y'all had dinner?" Taylor asked.

"No, we haven't, but we have a favorite place. Would you guys like to try it? We'll go Dutch," Lee said.

Taylor and Ed enjoyed the evening. He mused about enjoying the company of women who told him up front they wouldn't have sex with him.

Lee was a Louisiana girl, about five-four, with hazel eyes, brown hair, and an easy manner.

The evening went well, with conversation and alcohol dimming the ever-present thoughts and visions of the battlefield.

Lee and Taylor connected right away and spent the evening conversing about the war, home, and the future. They became good friends and saw each other often.

Referred to as the green zone, there were restaurants and bars they occasionally went to, but everyone preferred to hang out with Taylor and his buddies inside the base compound.

Everyone pitched in and bought food from the base PX and local markets.

Give him and his pals an hour or so with any mixed bag of food, and they would prepare a meal that would make you "slap your mama," as the guys liked to say.

And in the heavily guarded base, they didn't have to look over their shoulder every minute for the bad guys and could relax a little more.

Even then, weapons, for any eventuality, were close at hand in case the enemy made it inside the compound. Looking at the guys relaxing, playing football, or lifting weights, belied a sixth sense developed from being shot at too many times. They were keenly aware of their surroundings. If one guy saw or felt something was out of place, the platoon would go into combat mode in a heartbeat.

Women worked in every Military Occupational

Specialty (MOS) on the base: nurse, pilot, truck driver, mechanic, etc.

And there were the Long-Range-Recon guys (nickname LURPS) that went where no sane person would venture. They joked about being the archetype of the Catch-22 paradox. They would parachute into the middle of enemy territory. Then, with no backup, they would search for enemy forces that were usually multiple times the size of their seven-man team. They would call in air strikes and engage the enemy as if they were of equal size. Their death rate was the highest in the infantry cadre. They stood out because they didn't talk much and struggled not to be abusive in a social environment. They rarely let their guard down, but the camaraderie with Taylor and his buddies was one of those times they could unwind for a while, knowing they were among brothers.

***

A couple of weeks into their relationship, Taylor volunteered to drive Lee to a village a few miles out of town to treat the locals for their medical needs.

They were to return that same day, but an Al-Radea unit had been spotted in the area. The squad's sergeant, who escorted them to the village, received orders to stay there until a recon sweep of the area cleared out any enemy soldiers.

They were alone, sharing a mud-brick hut in the Iraqi desert. "It's going to be a long night. Would you like a drink?" he asked.

"Where are you going to find alcohol around here?"

"I'll check with the locals and see what I can find."

Thirty minutes later, he returned with four bottles of homemade beer. He went to their Humvee and returned with a small canvas bag and a fire extinguisher. He placed the bottles of beer in the bag and discharged the fire extinguisher into it. The CO_2 covered the beer with ice, dropping the temperature to near freezing.

He held a bottle out to her, "how about a cold beer?"

"Amazing, you guys never run into a problem you can't resolve," she said.

"Cooling warm beer is a serious problem," he said. They drank beer and talked. Their conversation kept Taylor's mind from wandering to gunfire, grenades, blood, death, and whether he would leave this place alive.

Wearing fatigue pants and a tee shirt, he was lying on his back in an Army cot, gazing at Lee standing in the doorway of their mud hut. Her body was silhouetted by the glow of a full moon. Finishing her beer, she retrieved two more from the bag. She handed him one and looked intently at him for a moment. "I'm engaged."

After a long pause, he changed to a sitting position on the side of his cot and took a sip of beer. "Well, that shoots the hell out of my fantasy," he laughed.

"I've been thinking about our relationship. I would like to have a relationship with you like you have with your buddies. A brother or sister that will always be there for you. Someone that will readily walk beside you into your worst nightmare," she said.

"I appreciate your honesty. It will take time for me

to mentally shift gears about how I think about you, but if good friends are my only option, I'll take it," he said.

Sitting on the small porch back-to-back, Lee held her beer over her shoulder for a toast, "to best buds."

Back at the base dispensary, she gave him a long, not-a-best-friend kiss before she got out of the Humvee. "Hang on to that," she said as she walked away.

Three days later, his platoon was evaluated as back to combat-ready status and moved out to a forward firebase.

He thought it best to let their relationship distance itself to that of good friends as they had proposed, so he kept his communication with her to a minimum.

CHAPTER IV

road patrol

It was dawn when Taylor's platoon rolled out of the base compound in two Humvees and two Stryker vehicles, all bristling with various weapon systems.

Their mission was to secure the road from their base to another base thirty miles from them.

Several ambushes and IED incidents have occurred in the last few weeks.

Starting a few miles out of their base, they found five IEDs buried in a five-mile stretch of the road. It was nerve-wracking for the platoon to watch their buddies find the devices with detectors and destroy them.

Taylor's buddy, Ed, and two other men were on point that day. The lieutenant rotated the point man positions among half the platoon because it was so dangerous, but the guys preferred Ed. They couldn't pinpoint the reason, but something about him made everyone feel more at ease. One soldier walked on either side of the road with Ed in the middle. They walked fifteen to twenty yards ahead of the convoy with the responsibility of not walking it into an ambush, sniper, or booby trap. Ed was uncanny at focusing on that sixth sense that told him when something wasn't right. The Grim Reaper followed their every step. Tomorrow would never come if they didn't find the IED buried in the road before one of the vehicles set it off or if one of them missed a buried anti-personnel mine and stepped on it.

walking on the razor edge of death heightens the senses
beer tastes like champagne
the sky is bluer
you savor the taste of the morning air

They stopped for the night, sat up a perimeter watch, and tried to relax as best they could, knowing the Al-Radea was watching them from the surrounding mountains.

On day two, they entered a village close to the road. The people in villages like this one were in a difficult situation. If they work with the coalition forces, the Al-Radea will punish them, and if they help the Al-Radea, the coalition will give them a hard time.

As they searched the village, an interpreter asked the elders what they knew about the activities of the al-Radea in their area. The elders never gave military information to the coalition. But on this day, they told the lieutenant about a group of aid workers who were helping the villagers with their medical needs when a band of terrorists kidnaped them and took them to their camp in the mountains.

A few days after the kidnapping, the elders were

shown a video of the terrorist beheading one of the aid workers.

CHAPTER V

rescue aid workers

Taylor's platoon was on their way to a village where a group of international aid workers were being held captive. They had been kidnapped by one of the most callous terrorist groups in the Middle East. A video of a worker being beheaded was streamed on the internet.

***

A Blackhawk Helicopter was carrying the Rangers to the village. It was midnight and thirty minutes before they arrived at their destination.

The helicopter was flying with its navigation lights off to prevent being seen from the ground. But, inside, the red glow of the door warning light was on, intensifying the fierce look of the soldiers with camouflage paint on their faces.

The platoon Master Sergeant stood and declared it was time for the ritual of the damned. He removed the cap from a canteen filled with a secret formula energy drink that looked like blood. Each man carried a metal shot jigger in his Molle pack for such junctures and good luck. The sergeant filled each container before reciting the platoon maxim, Strength and Honor. The platoon repeated the dictum. Each man covered the jigger with the palm of his hand, and gripping it with his fingers and thumb, slammed it against his buddy's body armor before downing the bloody concoction.

They weren't just the first platoon of the 75th Ranger Regiment, they were a band of brothers willing to die for their country and one another. They were a group of the most lethal warriors on the planet. They brought an adversary a level of ferocity that few could challenge.

Ropes were attached to a bar protruding from the exterior fuselage on each side of the helicopter. At the insertion point, the aircraft hovered thirty feet off the ground. The helicopter crew chief opened the doors and dropped the free ends of the coiled ropes to the ground. Then he signaled each soldier with a slap on the back to fast rope simultaneously down the ropes to the ground. It took less than sixty seconds for the eleven men to exit the helicopter.

On the ground, the men double-checked their equipment. Then, with night vision goggles and a GPS device, they made their way to the village a mile away.

Days earlier, the CIA had recruited a villager to provide information about the layout of the village, their daily routine, and the aid workers' location.

CIA operators had met with the Ranger's commanding officer and updated him on the situation. They informed him that an aid worker would be beheaded the following day.

The procedure was for the terrorist leader and

several soldiers to take a worker to a small knoll in the desert outside the village. There, the soldiers would set up a video camera to stream the gruesome event on the internet.

With hands tied behind his back, the aid worker would be forced to his knees in a place where the bare ground was discolored from the blood of earlier beheadings. The terrorist would talk at length while being streamed live on the internet. After his oration, he would approach the worker from behind and decapitate the individual with a long sword.

The platoon was divided into two squads of five and six men. A lieutenant would command the five-man squad and continue to the beheading site. A master sergeant would lead the six-man squad and make their way to the village where the rest of the aid workers were being held.

The undercover villager was instructed to tell the workers to lie flat on the floor when they heard the word "*down*" shouted.

It was midmorning when the terrorist leader and a number of his soldiers left the village with one of the aid workers. At the beheading site, with the video camera rolling, the terrorist gave his discourse about the evil aid workers indoctrinating the Iraqi people with western propaganda. Finished with his oration, he pulled his sword from his sash and approached the worker.

While planning the attack, the lieutenant had told his sniper, Taylor, not to kill the terrorist leader but to wound him. "I want to get eyeball to eyeball with the

S-O-B," he said.

A single shot rang out, and the terrorist leader fell to the ground from a bullet hitting him in the thigh of his left leg. The next instant, the Rangers opened fire on the rest of the enemy soldiers, killing them in seconds.

As planned, at the sound of the shots, the other squad of Rangers stormed the village gathering room where the rest of the workers were being held. The Rangers entered the room yelling, *down,* and, in a torrent of gunfire, killed the terrorist guards left standing.

Back at the beheading site, the lieutenant stood over the terrorist leader looking into his eyes as he lay bleeding to death from the sniper bullet severing an artery in his leg. The lieutenant picked up the terrorist's sword and touched the point to the guy's neck, drawing a trickle of blood, as if he were going to stab him. Instead, he slammed the sword against a rock, breaking the blade from the handle. He placed the pieces on the guy's chest. "Your last beheading, you bastard."

The revulsion for the terrorist was intense. After the guy's last breath. "Good shot Taylor, the son-of-a-bitch had time to think about going to hell," the lieutenant said.

The operation was a marked success. An entire terrorist cell was destroyed, and the surviving aid workers were rescued unharmed.

***

The platoon set up camp for the night with plans to

return to their base camp the following mourning.

On the road to their home base, they stopped for a break. Some guys used the vehicle's tires for a backrest. Others lay down in the shadows of the vehicles using their helmets for a pillow.

Out of nowhere, a single bullet ricocheted off one of the Humvees, and everyone scrambled for cover. "Where did that come from?" the lieutenant asked. One of the guys pointed to a rock formation a quarter of a mile away. "I think it came from there." Everyone started searching the rocky terrain with their binoculars, and after a few minutes, one of the guys spotted movement. "I see him," a soldier said. Everyone trained their binoculars on the area the soldier was pointing to.

"Y'all keep an eye on him while we set up the 50-Cal," the lieutenant said.

Taylor and Dean, the two platoon snipers, set up the weapon. Taylor manned the weapon while Dean sat up the spotting scope with an integrated range finder. With the enemy soldier in the crosshairs, Taylor adjusted the scope as Dean provided data from a ballistics calculator: wind speed and direction, muzzle velocity, bullet mass, shape, etc.

But the individual pulling the trigger was the most critical factor in making the shot. Taylor must have total control of all the physical factors: nerves, breathing, and concentration. After a deep breath and a relaxing exhale, Taylor pulled the trigger.

It took a little over a second for the 660-grain bullet to reach its target. "I see red," one of the guys snarled as he watched through his binoculars the Al-Radea soldier practically reduced to a bloody mist from being hit with a massive 50-caliber bullet.

"Dammit, Lawton, you were high and to the right a good inch. I ought to fire your ass," the lieutenant joked.

"Okay, men, load'em up, if we haul ass, we may get to sleep in our own bunks tonight," the Master Sergeant ordered as if the shot Taylor made killing an enemy soldier a quarter mile away was just another day at the office. The platoon completed its operation and returned to its FOB.

***

It had been two months since Taylor had seen Lee. He and a group of buddies were having a weightlifting competition. The guys had their shirts off and were sweating profusely as they worked with heavy weights. Taylor was straining to top the heaviest weight set by one of his buddies.

"Come on, Lawton, you can do it," a female voice said.

With the last ounce of strength, he made the press and looked to see who made the comment. It was Lee, "Hey," she said.

He was mystified. "How in the world did you get here," he said.

"One of your guys has appendicitis, and Liz, you remember her, was on Medevac duty when the call came in. She noticed it was your base and contacted me to see if I wanted to go in her place, so here I am. We will be leaving in a couple of hours. Is there someplace private we can talk?"

He brought a couple of glasses of tea from the cafeteria, and they sat at a picnic table. "I guess you're marking off the days on your short-timer calendar. I've seen some pretty bawdy calendars of naked girls with a month of days numbered on her, with the last three marked you-know-where. I want to see your calendar sometime," she said, recalling her impulsive act of sending him a nude photo of herself to use in his calendar.

"I almost had a heart attack when I received that photo," he laughed.

"I would never have had the nerve to do that under any other circumstance or less wine," she confessed.

They talked until the helicopter crew chief told her they were ready to leave. Two crew members carried the sick soldier on a stretcher while Lee walked alongside carrying IV bags. After securing the soldier in the chopper, she walked to Taylor. "Please be careful. I don't want to come back here and pick you up in a body bag," she said as she kissed him.

She walked away, then turned back to him and shouted over the noise from the helicopter. "I'm not engaged any longer. I'm in love with another man."

She didn't wait for a response but turned and boarded the helicopter. She waved to him from the open doorway as it lifted off.

CHAPTER VI

civilian life

After completing his time in Iraq, Taylor was going home. He boarded a C-17 transport airplane at the Mosul Airport that made a nonstop flight to McChord Air Force Base in Washington state.

Taylor was gazing out the taxi's window that was taking him into Tacoma to the first hamburger joint he saw when he noticed a Harley Davidson motorcycle parked up close to the highway with a for sale sign on it. The taxi was almost a mile past the bike before he asked the driver to turn around and return to the motorcycle.

A Hells Angel-looking guy approached him, and they shook hands. "Nice bike,." Taylor said.

"Yeah, I put a lot of elbow grease in that one. I've built several bikes, but this one turned out especially well," Kent the bike owner said.

Kent apprised Taylor in detail about the modifications he had made to the motorcycle. He started it and gestured for Taylor to take it for a test ride.

After running it through the gears down the highway, he pulled back into the yard. "This is one nice bike. What are you asking for it?"

"$16,500," Kent replied.

"Are you coming back from Mujiland?" Kent asked.

It was evident that Kent was ex-military by his speech and manner.

"Got off a C-17 about an hour ago."

"Infantry?" Kent asked.

"Yeah, 75 double R."

"In some bad shit?"

Taylor nodded affirmatively.

"Hell man, give me 15K."

Taylor and Kent worked out the details of how he would pay for the bike with nothing but a handshake.

He returned to McChord on his new bike, picked up his personal effects from the transit barracks, stuffed them in his duffle bag, and strapped it onto the motorcycle. He stopped at the discharge building to advise the Army he would not be continuing to Arkansas by military means but would go his own way from McCord.

Taylor felt weird riding down the highway without his battle rattle: weapon, backpack, helmet, goggles, etc.

He roamed around the Northwest for a couple of weeks before heading home.

Missoula, Montana: had a few beers and arm-wrestled a biker gang member in the Elkhorn bar.

Jackson Hole, Wyoming: rodeo, rock climbing, and trout fishing.

Ouray, Colorado: Ophir pass on a bicycle to get your heart rate up.

Pratt, Kansas: Little League baseball and pheasant hunting. And had a few beers after a day of trout fishing with newfound friends at Cotter, a favorite fishing spot on the White River. On down the road, he spent the night on the ground by a no-name creek in the Ouachita National Forest.

***

A platoon buddy, Jake Dolan, lived on a small farm a few miles outside of Rogers, Arkansas. He had been discharged from the Army a few months before Taylor and had told him to call if he was ever in the area. He was excited to hear from Taylor. He gave him directions to his place and invited him to stay a few days.

Jake was lying back in an old recliner on the covered front porch of his cabin. He was watching whitetail deer eat corn from a feeder when Taylor came riding up his driveway. "Hey man, is there a bar around here where a guy can get a cold beer?" Taylor joked. Jake threw him a beer from his cooler. "Taylor Lawton, how in the hell are you, buddy?" Jake asked as he gave Taylor a big bear hug.

They spent the next few hours bantering about war stories and life after the military.

Jake was a hard-core biker, and for the next few days, they rode the winding mountain roads of Northwest Arkansas and fished for trout in the White River.

They were at Jake's target range one afternoon,

with two of his buddies practicing their shooting skills in preparation for a competition later that afternoon. "Man, I really like this area of the state. It wouldn't take much for me to move up here," Taylor said.

"You're welcome to stay with me until you find a place."

"I'm going to seriously think about it," Taylor said.

After a few more days of hanging out with Jake, Taylor headed for home.

***

Settling back into civilian life, Taylor knew he needed to start thinking about a job. While in the Army, he often thought about what he would do for a living after his discharge.

While in high school and the year after graduating, he had worked for a construction company. He had a good working knowledge of heavy equipment and working with steel and concrete.

One day he went to the company he had worked for to discuss his employment. Everyone was pleased to see him and wanted to hear about his experiences in the Army. After an hour's visit, the owner invited Taylor for lunch at a nearby restaurant. After their meal, Taylor began to talk about his future. "I like the construction business. I was hoping to come back to work for you."

Junior Watson, the company owner, was silent for a moment. "I've been thinking about expanding my business into the Northwest part of the state. The area is growing like crazy. There is good money to be made up there, but my son and I have too much Ouachita River bottom mud on our boots to move. And it won't be long before I get serious about retiring anyway.

"I've been kicking around the idea of partnering with someone I can trust and isn't afraid of long hours and hard work. Then you walk in the door. I know your work ethic, and you're a quick learner. You were operating equipment like a pro in no time when you worked for me. I think you're the person I've been looking for.

"I was in Vietnam for thirteen months back in sixty-eight, so I know first-hand the life of a ground pounder. I'm sure you have experienced more of life in your time in the Army than most guys will encounter in their lifetime.

"If you're interested, I will finance the new operation and make you an equal partner. I will work and impart my knowledge of the business until you're ready to run me off to my fishing boat. Then, when I retire, my son will take over the south company, and I will sell my part of the northwest operation to you."

Taylor was shocked at the offer. "I don't know what to say. I am profoundly grateful that you would offer me this opportunity. I will work my ass off to grow the company."

Working from daylight to dark, sometimes in the dark, six days a week, Taylor learned every detail of the business.

He had been running the new company for eight months when his partner had an accident that forced him to retire early. His son took over the south company, and he sold his half of the north operation to Taylor.

***

A few months later, Lee's time in the military was up. They married and bought a house.

After two years of hard work, they were doing well enough financially to purchase a house on forty acres of land about ten miles outside the city. They remodeled the house and added an outdoor kitchen. They adopted two dogs from the local shelter and bought several cows and chickens.

When life couldn't get much better came that fateful day. They were in Oshkosh, Wisconsin, for the annual air show. They had flown there with friends who owned an airplane. They took camping equipment and set their tents under the airplane's wing.

They enjoyed viewing the airplanes and talking with the owners. They were admiring a WWI airplane when the owner approached. Lee was fascinated with vintage airplanes and asked if he ever took people for a ride. He told her he would be delighted to take her for a trip around the airport.

With a big smile, she waved from the open cockpit as they taxied to the runway and lifted off into the sky. They did several aerobatic maneuvers with no problems. Then as they were doing another maneuver, something went wrong, and the airplane slammed nose-first into the ground, killing her and the pilot.

The NTSB inspection determined a mechanical

failure occurred, making it impossible to control the airplane.

***

After Lee's death, he sold his business and farm and built a cabin and boat dock on the lake.

There was a sailboat club up the lake from his cabin. The club's private marina had fifty or so boats. He had friends who were members and had boats docked there. They often invited Lee and him to go sailing and taught them the sport's basics. They often volunteered as crewmen to help with the sails. The club regularly had races and other sailing competitions to improve their skill. They had vacationed with friends in the British Virgin Islands and rented a barefoot sailboat.

After Lee's death, their friends continued to include him in their social group. But he lightheartedly threatened to leave the group several times when they tried to help him find a girlfriend. "When you find a gal that knows how to operate a backhoe, field dress a deer, and drinks scotch whiskey straight, call me," he would laugh.

CHAPTER VII

hiking with friends

"Come on in, guys. The water is fantastic," Emily said. "Go on Les I want to take photos of y'all, and someone needs to keep watch for Bigfoot," Taylor said.

While everyone else was playing in the water, he picked up an armload of dead tree limbs and built a fire. After their swim, they gathered around the fire and opened a bottle of Peppermint schnapps for the occasion. They filled plastic cups for everyone and saluted their adventure. "This is so good when you're cold. It warms you down to your toes and other places," Emily said, giving her husband an amorous look. "Les, you may have some serious business to take care of when you get home," Taylor said. "If she has another one, it won't be at home, but the first place I can get off the road after we leave y'all," he said with a chuckle.

"You're embarrassing me," Emily said.

It was midafternoon when they returned to their vehicles, and everyone was hungry. "We need to hurry. The café closes at four," Taylor reminded them. They got into one vehicle because they were between the café and home and would return to their individual vehicles on their way back.

The quintessential mountain village of Kjolr, population ninety-six, was nestled deep in the Ozark mountains. It was the home of the Kjolr café and general store. Built-in 1890, the store was the destination for outdoor enthusiasts of every stripe. The store was the only business in town.

When they arrived, the dirt parking lot was full of bikers, which was not unusual because the winding mountain roads were a favorite to ride.

Most of the time, it was local folk: plumbers, bankers, and lawyers. But today, these guys were different. They wore leather jackets with a red devil on the back and the word Lucifer emblazoned on them. Taylor felt uneasy about the bikers as Les parked their vehicle and they went into the store. They had a pleasant meal and talked about their hike and next adventure.

When they exited the café, several bikers sat at a picnic table at the end of the store's covered porch. "Nice ass girlies, one of y'all want to ride on my hog?" one of the bikers remarked.

Taylor wasn't surprised. He was already 'locked and loaded'. "Hey man, we're not looking for trouble on such a beautiful day. If you would kindly apologize to these ladies for being a shit-for-brains moron, we will be on our way."

The biker stepped off the porch onto the dirt parking lot and gestured for Taylor to fight him. "I'm gonna kick your hillbilly ass before I take one of your gals for the ride of her life."

Taylor's uncle had taught him how to box, and the Army had taught him hand-to-hand combat. He worked out regularly in his home gym and a friend's boxing club.

"Taylor, please ignore him. Let's go," Emily said nervously.

He didn't respond to her but walked toward the biker. He could tell by the way the guy was standing he wasn't a boxer but a roundhouse brawler. The guy was bigger than him, but he figured as long as the guy didn't get him on the ground, he could probably whip him.

Taylor walked up to the guy and, without hesitation, jabbed him in the nose. When the guy tried to block the next jab, Taylor knocked him down with a hard punch to his jaw. Enraged, the biker got up and charged him. Anticipating the move, Taylor sidestepped the guy like a bullfighter and slammed his fist into the guy's temple, knocking him unconscious. He started to kick the guy in the throat, which could kill him, but he backed off.

Standing over the biker, he looked at the rest of the gang to see what would come next. Several bikers were surrounding him when the gang boss stepped forward. "Hold on, guys," he said as he walked toward Taylor but stopped a few feet from him with his hands up, indicating he didn't want to fight. "I saw a tattoo on your hand while you were fighting." The guy held his hand to Taylor, exposing the tattoo of a Viking sword between the thumb and forefinger of his right hand that was identical to the one on Taylor's hand. Surprised at the revelation, Taylor warily accepted the guy's extended hand, and they performed the Ranger's secret handshake. "75th Ranger Regiment," the boss said loud enough for his guys to hear as he held his hand up, showing his tattoo. "This is my brother. I will fight by his side until my last breath. If you fight him, you will fight me," he vowed as he looked with a wry frown at the guy on the ground, struggling to get back on his feet. "Jimbo, you picked the wrong dude to mess with. You're lucky to be breathing."

***

There was silence in the truck as they returned to their vehicles. "What's the next adventure on the list, sky diving?" Taylor remarked as if the incident had never happened.

"I thought you were going to kill that guy," Margret stammered.

Everyone was preparing to head home in their separate vehicles. "Les, I think I saw Emily taking another shot of that peppermint schnapps," Taylor said, trying to lighten the mood. The girls hugged him, and Emily sardonically remarked about his disposition. "We include you because you're such a party animal."

CHAPTER VIII

terrorist attack

Taylor was on his way home when his cell phone rang. It was another friend, "Jamie, what's up?"

"What are you doing?" Jamie asked.

"Just left Kjolr after a hike with Les, Margret, and Emily."

"Good for you. I should hang out with you more. I could use the exercise. Hey, I was checking to see if you were still planning to watch the game tomorrow at Lojos?"

"Looking forward to it," Taylor replied.

Lojo's restaurant and bar were in the basement of a building built in 1911. There was a short flight of stairs down to the entrance from the sidewalk. The atmosphere was warm and comfortable on this cold, damp afternoon. The original steam radiators provided the heat, complementing the ambiance of this classic restaurant and bar.

He and longtime friends were drinking beer and watching a pro football game. Several people with umbrellas shielding themselves from the misting rain walked past the window. Occasionally one would come into the bar. The bartender was conversing with a man and his wife sitting at the bar. Another group of people was playing darts.

"The Saints are looking good, and so is BJ," Bill, a good friend sighed as the waitress forty years his junior brought a pitcher of beer to their table. "You're looking pretty good yourself, William. Have you been fishing naked on your boat to get that tan?"

"I was just about to ask if you wanted to go fishing with me in your birthday suit," he replied.

"I agree. Their defense looks a lot better this year. It would be great if they could make it to the playoffs, and yes, BJ is looking beautiful as usual," Taylor said.

***

It was an idyllic atmosphere until the TV suddenly switched to a national news affiliate. A bomb had exploded in the international airport in New York. Eight people were dead, and many more were wounded. The Iraqi warlord Abdul-Hadi had taken credit for the attack and swore he would cleanse the earth of all infidels and create a worldwide Islamic caliphate.

Toby, another friend, cursed. "That son-of-a-bitch should be hung by his balls. I hope we find him quickly. If they would take me at my age, I would re-up in the Army, hunt down that piece of shit, and blow his brains out."

The news suddenly changed the mood in the bar. People were leaving in the middle of the game. He and his friends stayed for the game, but the enjoyment was gone. All they could talk about was the bombing. After his friends had left, Taylor moved to the bar. "Tommy, I'll have a scotch, please."

"It's hard to believe there are people in this world that think nothing of killing innocent people, even babies," Tommy lamented.

They talked for another hour about the bombing before Taylor left. At home, he could not stop thinking about the bombing. He turned on the TV and listened to the networks replay the event.

The following mourning, he was drinking coffee on his patio while watching squirrels run on top of his wooden fence. He was still thinking about the bombing. He dreamed about hunting the guy down and killing him.

He had joined the Army during the war in Iraq and had experienced several battles.

CHAPTER IX

plan adventure

It has been two years since the plane crash. He didn't have many obligations.

all I have to do is get off my ass and go for it
don't blow this off as a pipe dream

He spent a week researching online and watching international news to gather more information about what was transpiring in the middle east. He began to make plans for the adventure of a lifetime.

He knew the answer before he asked but inquired at the local recruitment office about returning to active duty. The guys were respectful, especially after reviewing his records. But they all knew the age limit regulation would not allow him to return to the Army.

He was out on his fishing boat trying to figure out the logistics of his dubious adventure. How to travel to Iraq was a primary concern. There were particular items he would like to take, and the anonymity he would prefer ruled out flying.

He kept thinking about his old Army buddy, Ed,

who had asked him many times to sail with him when he visited friends in Cyprus. He put his fishing rod down, retrieved a beer from his cooler, and called him.

After catching up since they last talked, he told Ed his plan. "Damn, Lawton, I haven't heard from you in over a year, then out of the blue, you drop this bomb on me. Are you calling me from a sanitorium? A million guys, including me, have watched this horrible attack on TV and daydreamed about going after this terrorist bastard. But the "balls to the wall," Taylor Lawton, I remember from the 75th, is having nothing to do with daydreaming.

"I'm preparing to go sailing with a pretty lady this evening and have dinner on my boat. Tomorrow I'm playing golf with friends, and afterward, drink some good scotch whiskey while playing poker. Then I'm going home to a nice comfortable house with air conditioning and clean sheets. I would be nuts to go with you on this crazy ass adventure. And on top of all that, I swore if I made it back home from our deployment over there, I would never go back. So, with that said, from one crazy person to another crazy person, sign me up. I was planning my yearly sailing trip to Cyprus pretty soon anyway, and adding this adventure will certainly heighten the anticipation of the voyage," he jested.

Taylor told friends he was sailing to Cyprus with an old Army buddy. "I'm meeting my buddy, Ed Marshall, at Harker's Island, North Carolina. We will sail from there.

***

He decided the best cover for him would be to pose as a freelance photojournalist. So, he had a local printing company make authentic-looking press badges, ID cards, and fake driver's licenses.

He was the yearbook photographer in high school and had helped edit the school newspaper, so he figured he could 'wing it' well enough to con most people. Also, being a freelance photojournalist would enable him to move around without too much scrutiny.

Walking down the marina dock and looking at the boats, he saw Ed waving to him. When he reached Ed's boat and came aboard, Ed gave him a big bear hug. "Man, you look well, all trim and tan."

"Thanks, you look the same as the last time I saw you except for those gray sideburns," Taylor joked.

"I was surprised to hear from you after all these years I've been trying to get you to sail with me. Then, out of the blue, here you are."

"What a beautiful boat. Is this the same one you bought after you left the service?" Taylor asked.

"Same boat with a few repairs and improvements over the years," Ed replied.

While Taylor stowed his gear, Ed started the diesel engine and cast off the dock lines from his 38-foot sailboat, "Solemate." They motored out of the bay, hoisted the sails, and heeled into blue water. Ed set a course for Bermuda and turned on the autopilot. He went below deck and returned with a bottle of scotch and glasses. He poured a couple of fingers into each glass and handed one to Taylor. They touched glasses saluting their adventure and talked into the sunset about their time in the military, family, work, and the future.

"I feel twenty years younger. It feels so right with the sun, wind, and ocean awakening your senses. I should have done this with you a long time ago. I had no idea what true, blue water sailing does for the soul." Taylor said after two days at sea.

After brief stops in Bermuda and Tarifa, Spain. They docked at a marina in Cyprus. A scenic bay protected it from the ocean waves by a manmade breakwater.

After securing the boat and talking with fellow sailors about the best bars and restaurants, they headed down the pier to a recommended bar. As usual, wherever sailboats congregate, the owners quickly become friends. They had planned to have dinner at a restaurant. But after meeting new seafaring friends at the bar, they were invited to a cocktail party with hors d'oeuvres back at the dock pavilion. They returned to the dock and joined the marina vibe.

CHAPTER X

Kathryn

After a few days of R&R Taylor went to the US Embassy. He wanted to contact the CIA to let them know his plans and hopefully get their approval and support. Taylor had worked with the CIA while in the Army and had become friends with several operators. He hoped referencing their names would improve his prospects for their support.

Soldiers in full battle gear guarded the receptionist area of the embassy. He had to show his passport, empty his pockets, and remove any metal items before going through a metal detector. Taylor requested to speak to a CIA staff member and referenced the names of the CIA operatives he knew. The receptionist called several departments, but no one could help him. He left the embassy dismayed.

He walked across the street to a restaurant with outdoor tables to have a drink and figure out another way to contact the CIA. He was drinking a Bloody Mary, people-watching, and daydreaming when he noticed a business-dressed woman coming from the embassy. She crossed the street and sat at a table close to him. The waiter brought her a glass of wine.

She didn't act like she was waiting for someone. Taylor watched her for quite a while. He feared making a scene and missing an opportunity at the same time. He approached her, "I saw you coming from the embassy. Do you work there?" he asked.

She looked up at him. "Why do you ask?"

"I'm a journalist. I just came from the embassy. I requested information about a recent terrorist attack to help me with an article I contracted to write for a newspaper in the US, but I couldn't find anyone to help me." Taylor said.

"You're an American?"

"Yes, I'm Taylor," he answered, extending his hand.

"Kathryn," she said as they shook hands.

"May I?" he asked as he put his hand on the back of the chair.

"You're ruining my break," she said.

"I'm sorry, but I really need help."

"What kind of help are you looking for?" she asked.

"Before I tell you that, will you please confirm that you work in the embassy?"

"I'm not an embassy employee. I work for an organization that has an office there," she answered.

Abruptly she stood, "I'm sorry, I can't help you."

"Please, don't leave. I understand your skepticism. How can I convince you I'm not a bad guy?"

After a long pause, she sat back down. "Give me your social security and military ID if you were in the military."

He wrote the numbers on a napkin and handed it to her. She took a photo of the numbers with her cell phone before shredding the napkin into small pieces and stirring them into her glass of water.

She stood up from the table and looked at her cell phone. "I don't know why I'm doing this but meet me here at three o'clock."

He aimlessly walked the streets full of vendors. He watched tourists negotiate the price for an endless array of merchandise while thinking about what he could say to Kathryn that might persuade her to help him with his venture. He knew he was grasping at straws but didn't see a lot of downside to the situation other than convincing this person that he was crazy.

Thirty minutes past their meeting, he began to think she was not coming when he saw her walking across the street.

"I'm sorry, my computer knew I was in a hurry and slowed to a crawl. I ran you through the US background analysis system. You are who you say you are, except for the journalist thing. I knew that was BS anyway," she said with a chuckle.

"I will say, after reviewing your records and combat experience, it makes you much more credible for consideration regarding whatever you're planning."

"Now, will you tell me who you work for?" he asked.

"I'm not comfortable disclosing that information at this time. You lied about being a journalist. You're off to a bad start," she said.

"It was a little white lie to get you to talk to me. I need someone to help me contact the CIA," he said.

"I was planning to only help you do that by introducing you to someone at the embassy who might help you, and that would be the end of it. I have a rule to not get involved with lost causes and crazy characters. But I'm intrigued after looking over your military record. So, I'm considering getting more involved in your venture until I confirm you are crazy. And buying me a glass of wine may help gain my support," she laughed.

"Great, I'm about to spill my guts to a woman I just met at a café, but you may be my best shot," he said.

She retrieved a small voice recorder from her purse and laid it on the table. "I would like to record our conversation to take notes and add to the dossier I have started on you. Are you okay with that?" she asked.

"I feel like I'm being interrogated about a crime," he answered.

"I haven't heard your proposal yet, but I get the impression it will be dangerous, and you want help from people who could get killed being involved. It is unlikely the people I take this venture to will even consider it, but if they do decide to help you, I want them to know what they're dealing with," she replied.

He disclosed his plan to Kathryn. "That is quite a scheme. Surely you know the odds of success in such an endeavor are right at zero. And the probability of you being killed is high, to say the least." She said.

Kathryn continued to interview Taylor. "Are you alone on this venture?"

"I have a friend with me. We were in the same outfit

in the Army. We traveled here on his sailboat."

"How involved will he be in your endeavor?"

"We haven't discussed the exact parameters, but I would say his primary involvement will be logistical but direct support when needed."

"What's his name?"

"Edward Marshall."

"Give me a few days to present this venture to the appropriate people to see if they have any interest in helping you. I will contact you with their decision."

The pavilion had an outdoor kitchen with a BBQ grill, fish cooker, and an eclectic mix of tables and chairs. There was an ice maker and a large cooler full of beer and wine. Ed's sailboat was in a slip a few yards from the pavilion where the sailing fraternity gathered every evening. They were cooking fish bought from a local boat a few hours earlier.

It had been a week since Taylor last talked with Kathryn when he received a call from her. "When can we meet?" she asked.

"I'm at the Meridian marina. Would you like to meet at the marina bar?" he asked.

"I would like to meet your friend, Ed. I need to talk with him if he is involved in this venture. I am familiar with the Meridian Marina. Give me your dock and slip number."

Kathryn came aboard Ed's boat, and Taylor introduced her to Ed. "Hello Ed, nice to meet you. What a beautiful boat. I occasionally sail with friends, and I love it," she said.

"Would you like a drink?" Taylor asked.

"White wine, please. I know red wine and white sailboats don't go together very well," she joked.

The formal meet-and-greet conversation became more relaxed as they explored their new relationship.

She requested Ed's social and military ID numbers. "How do you plan to get to Iraq?" she asked.

"We plan to dock Ed's boat in Lebanon." From there, it's a crap shoot. Hopefully, that's where the CIA will help.

"Is Ed going to Iraq with you?" she asked.

"No, he may stay in Lebanon for a few days, but he will return to Cyprus. He will handle logistics and be on standby when I get in a bind," Taylor said.

"And he is damn good at getting into them. You notice he didn't say if," Ed said.

"Are there weapons on the boat?"

"Yes," Taylor said.

"Lay them out where they can be seen, don't try to hide anything. I will arrange for customs to expect you. Give this envelope to the boat captain when they come aboard." she said.

"If that wraps up our business, I invite you to join Ed and me for an evening cruise. We have wine and cheese," Taylor urged.

She took a moment to consider his offer. "I'm breaking rule after rule dealing with you, Mr. Lawton, but I can't resist the offer of wine and cheese," she said.

The sail was a good ice breaker for everyone, each tempering their business persona with a little help from the wine. Kathryn eagerly helped with the sails, as directed by Ed, and took the helm for a time. Upon returning to the dock, Kathryn stayed and ate the fish Taylor and Ed had prepared earlier. "What a pleasant evening. Thank you so much for inviting me to sail with you. I must go now, as I have work to do on your behalf."

Taylor didn't want her to leave but resisted trying to convince her to stay.

CHAPTER XI

CIA

Ed made minor repairs to his boat while Taylor bought provisions. They were ready to leave for Lebanon.

Upon entering the designated control area, Ed contacted the harbor patrol. They told him to lower the sails and wait for customs. Within a few minutes, a patrol boat pulled alongside them, and a crewman threw a line to Ed for him to tie the boats together. The harbor patrol officials were expecting them. Three customs officials came aboard. "Your passports and boat registration, please, and permission to search your boat."

As the officials searched the boat, Taylor handed one of them the envelope Kathryn had given him. After a few minutes of looking over the documents, the official returned to the patrol boat and gave them to an individual who looked like she was the commanding officer. Taylor could see her talking on the ship's marine radio.

Thirty minutes later, the officials returned to their boat. "Follow us."

Ed started the engine and followed the patrol boat. Passing docks full of power and sailboats, they continued to a smaller dock separate from the others. Communicating by two-way radio, Ed was instructed to dock his boat and wait for further instructions.

After waiting an hour, they were surprised to see Kathryn and a man walking down the dock toward them. Kathryn and her companion boarded Ed's boat, "Taylor, Ed, this is Matt." Taylor surmised Matt was CIA.

After a period of general conversation, Matt began discussing Taylor's endeavor.

"When Kathryn first approached me with your plan, I thought it implausible. Then Kathryn told me about your relationship with some of our special forces people while you were in the US Army. Of the names you gave Kathryn, I contacted two of them, and they both spoke highly of you. But even with their recommendation, I wasn't convinced that we should get involved in your venture. But Kathryn pressed me to consider your plan from an operator's perspective. She insisted we challenge our standard operating procedures in evaluating your proposal.

"After reviewing your military records and more discussion, the result was basically, what do we have to lose? We haven't been able to find the murdering son-of-bitch on our own, and a covert operator does have its advantages. And what if he were to pull this off with some help from us and kill this Abdul-Hadi bastard," Matt said with disgust.

The following morning Taylor and Kathryn met at

a bakery in the marina to discuss the meeting with Matt, "How do you feel about the meeting?" she asked. "It went well. Thank you for your help. I see now that I would have gotten nowhere with the CIA on my own," he said.

"Our coincidental meeting could benefit all the parties involved in this endeavor. We may thank you sometime in the future," she said.

"A full background check was run, and both of you have been approved for the Private Military Contractor classification. It was noted that you both had the top-secret classification in the Army, so it was a matter of updating your files.

"A security clearance is necessary because you will be going to facilities and dealing with people and organizations that require a security clearance. I will take you to these facilities as soon as the paperwork has been approved.

"Meanwhile, I want to reciprocate to Ed and you for inviting me to go sailing. I socialize with a group of friends who occasionally take turns having happy hour at our residences whenever we are all in town at the same time. One is taking place this evening, and I invite Ed and you to go with me."

The occasion was in an apartment overlooking a manicured green space. A large balcony afforded a panoramic view of the city. There were walking paths with metal benches. In the center of the piazza was an abstract sculpture of sea creatures spewing water from their mouths into a circular pool.

Kathryn's friends were an eclectic troupe that

covered the social spectrum from army private to embassy director.

She joined Taylor on the Veranda. "Well, what do you think of this motley crew?"

"First, let me tell you that for some weird reason, I especially enjoy events like this where I don't know a soul. Isn't that crazy?" he said.

"No, it's not, considering you're not afraid of Godzilla and couldn't care less what people think of you," she said.

"How did you determine my disposition so quickly? Are you a shrink among your other attributes?" he asked.

"But to answer your question regarding your friends, I enjoyed every conversation, especially with the gal who looks like a Sports Illustrated model."

She gave him a playful punch in the chest.

The taxi let the guys off at the marina. Taylor bent down to the vehicle's window, "It was an interesting evening. Thanks for the invitation."

"I'm glad you enjoyed it. Hopefully, I will hear from the office in the next few days regarding your venture. I will call you as soon as I hear from them."

A week later, Kathryn contacted Taylor, advising him that the authorization to proceed with their plan had been approved. She picked him up at the marina and drove to the embassy. They parked in the underground garage. But instead of going to the elevator, they entered a locked door that looked like a utility and storage room. Obscured by shelving and miscellaneous items was another elevator. After facial recognition access, they entered a subterranean complex of offices and workspaces.

Kathryn introduced Taylor to the people he would be working with.

After weeks of working with a group of special equipment people, they had built a camera and tripod system integrated with a laser designator and firearm, all cleverly hidden in the photography equipment.

Taylor was prepared. The time had come.

CHAPTER XII

Al-Radea operative

Today he would start his quest to kill Abdul-Hadi. With the help of a CIA social media specialist, Taylor had been corresponding with an Al-Radea principal named Shilam al Bekhamn for two months. Taylor portrayed himself as a photojournalist wanting to interview Abdul-Hadi.

The plan was to use Shilam to get to Abdul-Hadi. Slowly, over months of conversing with him, he had convinced Shilam that he wanted to help the American public better understand the Iraqi culture. Shilam had agreed to meet with Taylor and discuss the parameters of an interview with Abdul-Hadi.

The meeting with Shilam would take place at a business in Mosul.

Taylor informed Kathryn that he was ready to go to Mosul.

"I will have a car pick you up tomorrow at 0900 and bring you to the airport. Check-in at the corporate aviation office and ask for me."

Arriving at the facility the next morning, he

followed her instructions. The person he spoke with said they were expecting him. He was led through the office and hanger to the tarmac parking area. His guide pointed to an airplane a few yards away. "Have a good day," she said as she left him.

A portable ground power unit was hooked up to the airplane to power the aircraft without the engines running. The navigation lights and the air-conditioning system were on. Taylor walked to the aircraft and stuck his head in the airplane's open doorway, "Anyone home?" he asked.

"Hey, Lawton, come aboard." Taylor climbed the steps and entered the airplane. Kathryn was sitting in the pilot's seat. "Store your gear in the back and come up front," she said.

He stowed his bags and entered the cockpit to see Kathryn twisting knobs, pushing buttons, and talking pilot jargon with the control tower through a headset. "You are a remarkable woman. What new skill will I see tomorrow? How long have you been flying?" he asked.

"Six years ago, I was on an airplane two or three times a week because of my job, so I got to know the CIA pilots. On occasion when I was the only passenger on the airplane, the pilot would invite me to sit in the copilot's seat when a copilot wasn't required for that particular flight or aircraft.

"On a flight one day, the pilot was answering my question about flying. To help explain the answer, the pilot had me take the control wheel for a few minutes. I was instantly hooked and started taking flying lessons. After getting my private pilot's license, my boss liked the idea of my being able to fly the "Company" airplanes. So, he sent me to the US to further my training and get the type ratings required to fly a couple of different airplanes. I have logged about 2500 hours of flying time over the last three years. So, if you're brave enough to be my copilot, buckle up, and we'll burn some kerosene."

After landing in Mosul, Kathryn spent a few hours with Taylor before returning to Beirut. They took a taxi to his hotel to leave his gear before they went to a restaurant for dinner to further discuss Taylor's plan.

**

It was strange returning to Mosul. When he left, he was sure he would never return. So much had changed. The atmosphere was almost normal, but he knew that could change at any time.

To meet with Shilam, a procedure was agreed upon to make it safe for both parties.

His first step was to wait at a particular sidewalk café for further instructions. Taylor approached the restaurant and observed the area for a few minutes, looking for anything suspicious. He continued to the restaurant, sat at a table with an unobstructed view of the area, and ordered coffee.

The waiter brought his coffee and handed him an envelope. Inside was a note detailing the next step to follow. He was to walk to a specific outdoor shop and inquire about a particular camera. He found the shop and again watched from a distance for a good thirty minutes before he entered. After a few minutes of casually looking at the camera section, the proprietor asked if he could help him. Taylor told him he was looking for a particular camera. The proprietor asked if he had the model number. Taylor gave it to him. The proprietor gestured for him to follow him to the back of the store. From there, he was directed to take the stairs to a room over the shop.

Taylor took the stairs to a small room. There were rugs and cushions to sit on arranged in the middle of the floor. He was looking at the room when he heard someone coming up the stairs. He was expecting a typically dressed Iraqi, but this person was dressed in military fatigues and wearing a black Chitrali cap.

"Are you Shilam al Bekhamn," Taylor asked.

Shilam didn't acknowledge his question but gestured for him to sit.

To show he was not so eager for the interview that he was willing to kiss ass, he angrily exploded, "I will stand. I'm not interested in any posturing bullshit. All I want from you is to help set up an interview with Abdul-Hadi that will, hopefully, benefit both of us. If that isn't what you have in mind, I will walk out of here right now," Taylor snarled.

After a long silence, Shilam smiled. "I think we are going to have a good relationship."

The proprietor of the store entered the room. "You must be searched for weapons," Shilam said.

Taylor didn't resist the storekeeper frisking him for weapons.

"Please, sit with me. I don't like looking up at the person I'm talking with. Have some tea," Shilam said.

Poured from the same pot, Taylor waited for Shilam to take the first drink.

"I suggest we start our conversation with your telling me what I must do to interview Abdul-Hadi. If your demands are unreasonable or more than I can accomplish, let's not waste each other's time. I have a limited time to deliver a story to my editor. I have alternatives I can move to if we can't come to terms," Taylor said.

Again, Shilam ignored him. "I have a few questions, and we need to discuss the interview details," Shilam said.

Taylor had spent hours rehearsing this situation. He answered every question Shilam asked and repeated the answer when Shilam tried to trip him up. After a lengthy question-and-answer period, Shilam was satisfied with Taylor's responses, and they agreed upon the interview format. "I am satisfied with our meeting. I will make arrangements to proceed with the interview. Three days from today at 09:30 hours, a driver will pick you up at the train station in Erbil," Shilam said.

CHAPTER XIII

odyssey to the terrorist camp

Kathryn made arrangements to have Taylor transported to Erbil.

The first thing Taylor had to do when his driver arrived was to put his cell phone in a metal-lined box so it couldn't be tracked. That was one of the terms he had agreed to when he met with Shilam.

The driver didn't speak English, but his body language implied he didn't like the American. After loading his gear into the truck's bed, they headed toward the mountains. There was silence except for the road noise.

He felt the odds of his making it out of this place going against him each mile they traveled deeper into Al-Radea territory.

As they continued their journey, Taylor took photos of the changing landscape as they drove higher into the mountains. The driver didn't say anything about taking photos, so he continued photographing the landscape to possibly be able to later identify their location.

It was getting dark when the driver pulled off the road and stopped at a primitive campsite that was once a homestead. Nothing was left but a ring of stones for a campfire and a working water well for people traveling through the area.

Four lean-to-style shelters were made of large tree branches lashed together and attached to a tree. A tarp could be stretched over the branches to provide protection from the elements.

The trees provided fallen branches for firewood. The driver stacked wood in the fire ring and started a fire. He and Taylor went about securing their individual shelters and preparing a meal. The driver had a metal lunch box of food, and Taylor had an MRE.

After eating, Taylor went to his lean-to shelter and spread a tarp over the tree limbs. He rolled out his sleeping bag and made a pillow with his backpack.

Inside his sleeping bag, he contemplated what tomorrow would bring. The sky had more stars than he had ever seen.

A few minutes before dawn, Taylor was awakened by the driver loading his gear into his truck. After loading his gear, Taylor returned to the fire and made a thermos of coffee. He took a cup from a holder on the truck's console, filled it with coffee, and handed it to the driver, but he refused. He tried again, and he grudgingly took the coffee.

After five hours of steady driving, only stopping to get rid of the coffee, they reached the entrance to a narrow canyon. The driver stopped the truck, got out, stretched, and walked over to a flat rock. He lit a cigarette and sat down on the rock while Taylor stayed in the truck taking photos of the driver and the landscape.

Forty-five minutes had passed before a vehicle creating a dust trail appeared from the canyon. A white Mercedes SUV covered in dust pulled up and stopped a few yards away. A guy dressed in typical Iraqi attire got out of the driver's side. Another similarly dressed guy exited the passenger side carrying an AK47 rifle. The two men walked to the driver and talked for a few minutes.

Taylor had gotten out of the truck and was leaning against the hood when the two men approached him.

"I must search your bags and equipment," one of them said in broken English. He lowered the truck's tailgate and began to go through Taylor's bags.

"Give me your camera and jacket," the bodyguard said. Taylor complied, and the guy removed the memory card from his camera. He found another memory card in Taylor's camera bag. "You must give me all of your memory cards."

"That's all of them," Taylor said.

"Your person must also be searched for weapons and electronics."

Satisfied that he had nothing on his body that could compromise their leader, the men talked with the driver a few minutes before he departed in his truck.

Taylor's bags and equipment were loaded into the SUV. He was directed to sit in the front passenger seat and put a blackout mask over his eyes. The guy with the rifle sat in the rear passenger seat behind him.

After an hour of driving, they stopped and exited the SUV. Taylor was allowed to remove the mask covering his eyes. They had arrived at a village on a river about seventy yards wide. The village had four mud brick huts with thatched roofs and a large, covered pavilion.

The women were gathered on the bamboo deck of the pavilion. Some were repairing fishing nets while others prepared a meal. Several dogs were asleep under the deck in the cool shade. A flock of chickens was scratching the dirt for anything edible. The children were at the river, diving off a dock and swimming. The older ones were fishing from the bank a few yards away. Two fishing boats were pulled up on the sandy bank.

An old 30-foot coal-fired, open-bow steam-powered boat was tied to the dock. Taylor was intrigued when he noticed the boiler had the date 1912 on the manufacturer's production plate. When he inquired about the craft, one of the bodyguards said it was the boat in the movie, "The African Queen."

As he explored the boat, he chuckled at the unlikely prospect that Katharine Hepburn and Humphrey Bogart had been on the boat.

It was too late in the day to continue the trip. Taylor was directed to one of the huts where he would sleep. He brought his gear and prepared his sleeping bag. He was about to open an MRE for dinner when a bodyguard invited him to eat with them.

Everyone in the village had gathered at the pavilion for dinner. He was surprised to see the floor covered with bowls of food. A villager covered a large piece of flatbread with fish and vegetables. She handed it to Taylor and welcomed him with the palms of her hands held together.

After dinner, the men retired to the dock to smoke the Hookah and drink Brandy. Taylor joined them, musing over the circumstances that had brought him to this place.

It was a few minutes before sunrise. There was a layer of fog drifting on the surface of the river. Taylor was lying on his sleeping bag, watching a school of fish break the placid surface of the river.

He gathered his gear and walked to the dock. The village men had fired the steamboat boiler furnace. Smoke was coursing from the stack.

He stowed his gear on the boat and joined the men having breakfast.

Underway with two village men operating the boat, Taylor and the two bodyguards relaxed on cushions and drank coffee.

An hour into the trip, they came upon a fishing boat with a thatched roof covering half of it. Three men and a woman had stretched a net across the river to catch fish. One man waved for them to slow down so they wouldn't damage their net.

Upon slowing their boat, another boat appeared and raced toward them. The bodyguards grabbed their weapons and positioned themselves to fire. Taylor was told to stay at the stern of the boat and lay on the floor.

"Pirates," the bodyguard exclaimed.

A pirate sprayed a twenty-round magazine of bullets into the water close to Taylor's boat and demanded they surrender.

One of the bodyguards told the pirates who they were and angrily cursed them. He told them Abdul would hunt them down and hang them. After talking amongst themselves for several minutes, the pirates begged for forgiveness and asked permission to retreat. A bodyguard told the men in the fishing boat to cut the net down and leave the area with the other boat.

"We will tell Abdul about this. He will be angry that these men are robbing people in his territory. They will wish they had never entered our province after Abdul catches them," a bodyguard said.

The confrontation with the pirates had taken up the afternoon. With only an hour before dark, they decided to set up camp for the night. They tied the boat to a tree and were unloading their gear for the night when they heard another watercraft coming down the river.

Not knowing whether friend or foe, the men readied their weapons.

The boat was going fast when the occupants spotted their boat and stopped. A soldier jumped behind a machine gun mounted on the boat's front deck.

Both sides began looking at one another with binoculars. A guy on the boat spoke through a loudspeaker, "Do you speak English?"

"I'm American, and there are four Iraqis with me,"

Taylor shouted. After a few minutes, the boat slowly motored toward them with soldiers manning two machine guns, ready to fire if they were attacked. When they moved closer, Taylor could see they were US soldiers. "What are you doing with a boatload of rag heads," he demanded.

Kathryn had given Taylor a military identification code for situations like this. He wasn't to discuss or answer any questions regarding his status. Just provide the code to the person in charge. The person would log into a military server and enter the code. There were no details about the person, only another code that classified the individual's status.

The soldier ran the code Taylor gave him. He looked at Taylor. "What's your name?"

"Taylor," he responded. The soldier didn't press him for his last name. "Taylor, I think we're good and will be on our way."

They broke camp early the next morning and were on the river at first light. After four uneventful hours of steady steaming, they reached Abdul's camp.

The boat captain pulled alongside a dock on the river and tied the boat to it. The bodyguards and Taylor unloaded their gear and released the boat so the villager crew could return home.

They made their way up a well-worn path and through an opening between two rock formations.

They came to the entrance of a cave. There was nothing man-made to indicate the cave was inhabited by anything other than wild animals.

One of the men entered the cave and reappeared

after a few minutes, accompanied by another man. It was Abdul-Hadi.

CHAPTER XIV

the terrorist leader

Abdul approached Taylor and gestured for him to follow. "Come, have some tea," as he directed Taylor to a large rug with numerous cushions arranged for sitting. They were just inside the cave entrance out of the sun.

"Would you care to smoke?" as he motioned toward a Hookah pipe. "I have never tried it."

"You will like it."

Abdul instructed him on how to smoke it properly.

The person he was having tea with was not the person he envisioned. He was expecting a harsh, callous demeanor. Instead, he was quite civil.

this guy is playing a head game with me
I will roll with wherever he wants to go with this charade

Abdul talked about life in the abstract. It was apparent he was a shrewd individual. Taylor was already worried about his ability to convince Abdul that he was a journalist. He had to assume Abdul could read English, so he must write as well as possible if he was forced to show his work.

Eager for the interview and planning to kill Abdul at the first opportunity would be challenging. He was ready to proceed with the interview, hoping Abdul would inadvertently say something that could help him with his plan to kill him. But he concluded he should let Abdul initiate the discussion.

Abdul stood up and directed his men to take care of Taylor. "It is time for prayer. When I return, we will eat, then talk."

While Abdul was gone, Taylor made notes about their meeting. He was writing when one of the bodyguards brought him his camera. "Follow me, and I will show you to your quarters."

Taylor laid his bags down in a room off the main corridor of the cave. He looked over his camera to see if it was working properly and noticed all his photos had been deleted from the memory cards.

After prayer, Abdul came to him, "Come, I will show you my home away from home."

Taylor followed him into another part of the cave. They entered a large room with sunlight and a waterfall streaming through an opening in the stone ceiling. The water fell into a pool created by thousands of years of water eroding the limestone. "The water is beautiful and clean, a gift from Allah," Abdul said.

Two Asian women appeared from nowhere. "Bathe in the pool and leave your clothes on the stone," Abdul said.

When in Rome …

The pool and waterfall were amazing. Taylor had assumed it would be forever before he would enjoy a shower after leaving Cyprus. Leaving his clothes for cleaning, he wrapped a large towel around himself and returned to where he had left his gear. He wore clean clothes from his duffel bag.

A tent had been set up outside the cave. Inside, the traditional rugs and cushions were arranged.

Abdul was waiting for him. "Bring your camera and come with me." They walked a natural stone path up to a knoll directly above the cave entrance overlooking the river winding through a valley of multicolored rock formations.

Overlooking the valley was a thatched roof pergola with a handmade table and chairs. Beyond the pergola, a precipice protruded out from the cliff wall. There was a prayer blanket lying on the outer edge of the formation.

The sun was sinking below the horizon, and the sky was ablaze with the colors of a rainbow but more intense. "Wow, amazing," Taylor said as he took photos of the scenery. Abdul retrieved a bottle of liquor and glasses from a cabinet inside the pergola. "It has been a long journey for you. This is a beautiful brandy made in Iraq. It is better than the French Cognac," Abdul said as he poured each a glass. Taylor took a sip, "I don't know much about brandy, but this is indeed good." Abdul opened a box of cigars, "This will enhance the taste of the brandy," he said.

"I live a simple life that exemplifies the warrior spirit. From that perspective, it makes me humble but passionate about my relationship with Allah. But I beg a few pleasures of life," he said as he lit their cigars and took a sip of brandy. "Tell me about yourself, Taylor. Knowing a little about you may help me better understand the objective of our interview."

"In any other interview, I would counter that I am the journalist, and the interview has nothing to do with me. I'm simply recounting my experience for the reader. But I recognize the peculiar circumstance," Taylor said.

He talked at length about his past, focusing on his personal life. He told Abdul he was a journalist in the Army.

"Is it true you can have only one wife in the US?" Abdul asked.

"Yes, just one. In the US, they will put you in jail for having more than one. That is if your wife doesn't shoot you first."

"Tell me more about American women," Abdul said.

"Trying to enlighten you about the psyche of the American woman at this particular time may make your head explode. American women are revolutionizing their place in our culture as we speak. When they ultimately find their utopia, I hope they will still have some affection for men," Taylor quipped.

"I don't understand." Abdul said.

"Welcome to the club," Taylor joked.

Knowing the infinite difference in the societal status of American and Iraqi women, Taylor strove to enlighten Abdul as best he could on the subject.

"You chose the most difficult of subjects," Taylor said.

"Yes, they are a mystery," Abdul said.

After an hour of wide-ranging getting-to-know-you conversation, "It has been a long day for you. We will return to the cave, and you can retire to your quarters for the night."

Abdul was right, comfortably in his sleeping bag, he was asleep within a few minutes. When he woke, it was eerily quiet and so dark he could barely see the surrounding area. He had slept so soundly he was confused for a moment about where he was.

CHAPTER XV

He lay in his sleeping bag, reviewing his conversation with Abdul and preparing to be a journalist.

Abdul was waiting for him in the tent. "My beautiful girls have prepared a meal." He gestured for Taylor to sit with him as he held up a small cup. "Espresso at sunrise in the cool desert air is a beautiful thing."

"I agree," Taylor replied as one of the girls handed him a cup. After their meal and pleasant discourse, "Come with me, I will show you my little kingdom," he said.

A thirty-minute drive from the cave, they entered a narrow passage between two mountains. After a short drive, they entered a small canyon. From there, they drove up a perilous winding road cut into the side of the mountain. The single lane barely accommodated the vehicle. The tires were inches from the shear drop-off of a thousand-foot ledge. "If you're trying to scare me, it's working," Taylor exclaimed as he watched the tires of the vehicle roll inches from the edge of the cliff, making rocks fall down the side of the mountain. The slightest mistake and they would slide off the road into the canyon. "Malia is a good driver. He has driven this road many times. There are roads much worse than this. I will take you on one of them some time," Abdul said.

They left the vehicle at the top of the mountain pass and walked another quarter mile to a small plateau with a panoramic view of the area. Abdul pointed out villages and landmarks that made up his province.

After the tour they returned to the cave and continued their conversation on the knoll.

Abdul was reflective as he stood dangerously close to the edge of the sheer rock formation looking out over the valley with his back turned to Taylor, "I wonder if Allah is listening to our conversation. Do you entertain such thoughts, or am I mad?" Abdul mused.

"Each mile I traveled on the way here, I questioned my sanity," Taylor replied.

"To better understand the goal of our interview give me your perception of my beautiful country that is fighting for its very existence?" I will return you to Erbil regardless of your commentary," Adul said.

Taylor took a moment to consider Abdul's request. "Not having to measure every word as to how it might affect my well-being will certainly allow me the freedom to speak candidly. I am going to trust that you will honor your pledge. I will speak as I would to another journalist," Taylor said, reinforcing Abdul's words.

"I want you to enlighten me over the time we collaborate on this story and perhaps change my perception of your people."

"Ever since the advent of the opposing factions of Sunni and Shia, I see a culture that has been in a state of conflict for centuries and continues today. With the country divided, certain people seized the opportunity to become leaders of the opposing factions. Your culture is being used by these people to preserve their power. Each side has been indoctrinated with a single-minded ideology. Your people have little knowledge outside their forcefully controlled world. They are ideological believers. Thinking for oneself is forbidden.

"And determined to control the flow of oil and convert your country to an egalitarian state, the Western powers have poured gasoline on the conflict by sending their military forces into your country," Taylor said.

There was frustration on Abdul's face. "You are an infidel bastard. When we return to the tent, I will tell you what I think of your America, shoot you in the head with my pistol, and leave your carcass in the desert for the scavengers to eat," Abdul cursed.

Trusting he was being metaphorical, Taylor continued. "Before you do that, let me say that my present understanding of your cultural internal power struggle bears a similar discord to the enmity in the US. One could equate the Sunni versus Shia dispute with the dissension between the conservative and liberal factions in the US that have us at each other's throats. Our young people are being indoctrinated by an education system and social media network that wants to radically change our culture and government. They are zealously attacking our constitution and most cherished rights that have been paid for with the blood of untold patriots. Capitalism and individualism have become dirty words," Taylor groused.

"Now that I have stated my assessment of Iraqi culture based on information I garnered through personal observation and objective research, I am eager for an Iraqi native to enlighten me about their culture from their day-to-day life experiences," Taylor said.

"I must take a walk to temper my anger and the inclination to tell you to leave and go to hell," Abdul growled.

On his return, Abdul walked to the edge of the precipice and gazed out over the countryside. He appeared to be in deep thought. Finally, he turned to Taylor, somewhat composed.

"You think all Muslims are fanatical Islamists, but we are not of some mechanical dogma. Fifteen years ago, that may have been true, but with the death of Saddam Hussein, technology and information couldn't be suppressed any longer. The people of Iraq could see the real world. I am a good example, and what I am about to say will shock you. It shocks my sensibilities for the words to come out of my mouth when such thoughts have been only that, until now.

And to confess this to an infidel that I just met, and don't like, is surely a sign of my madness.

"I am agnostic about a number of the tenets of my faith but have absolute faith in Allah. I know Allah. I follow the tradition of daily prayer, but all I ever asked is for him to enlighten me as to the path he would have me follow that would please him. I read the Quran with logical conviction, so I always have more questions than answers."

CHAPTER XVI

concubines

When they returned to the tent, the SUV was there with the two bodyguards. One spoke privately with Abdul. "I must leave, you will be safe," Abdul said as he climbed into a vehicle with his bodyguards and drove away.

Taylor was taken back by this sudden development and felt uneasy being left alone with the two women he could hardly communicate with.

After their heated conversation, he needed a drink. Instead of waiting for them to bring him something, he followed the women to a large walk-in structure made of concrete with a blast-proof door. It looked like it was designed as a bomb shelter. The shelves were stocked with everything needed to survive for an extended period of time. In the back was a cabinet with a well-stocked supply of liquor. Taylor would normally look for scotch, but a cold beer was on his mind. Inside the naturally cool cave was a solar-powered refrigerated walk-in cooler. Upon entering the cooler, he found food, water, and cases of

American soft drinks and beer.

He opened three beers and handed one to each girl. They laughed and acted like they were drunk after one beer.

Having his second beer, he gestured to the women that he wanted to take photos of them. At first, they were hesitant to comply, as he directed them to the stone pool inside the cave.

The sunlight shining through the gap in the stone ceiling created an affable texture for a good photograph. They whispered to each other, giggled, and started taking their clothes off. Taylor shook his head and waved his hands to stop them from undressing. The women wanted to please him and, misinterpreting his gestures, continued to remove their clothes. He finally convinced them to keep their clothes on and laughed to show he wasn't angry. Taylor became engrossed in the moment as he positioned them in the pool and took photos in various poses. He had them submerge themselves in the water before having them sit at the pool's edge. With their long black hair and ankle-length white linen dresses clinging to their wet bodies, he photographed them in numerous postures. The women began to relax and enjoy him taking their photographs.

He was so absorbed in photographing the women that he didn't realize Abdul had returned. "Are you enjoying my beautiful girls?" Abdul asked. "Yes, women are a favorite subject," he said, laughing. Abdul spoke to the women, and they recounted their misunderstanding with Taylor. "Continue with your photography while I change my dusty clothes. Enjoy the girls. Meet me at the tent when you are finished."

Abdul was smoking a Hookah when Taylor entered the tent. "The girls are pretty, yes?"

"They are pretty, and while on that subject, I am curious about their status. How did they get here, and can they leave if they want to?" Taylor asked.

"You think the girls are here against their will, but your preconceived assumption is wrong.

"Two years ago, a unit of my soldiers ambushed a band of outlaws that were attacking villages in my province. My men attacked the outlaw camp one night and killed them. Searching through their tents the next morning, they found the girls.

"Unable to communicate with them, the commander brought them to me. When I first saw them, they were in pretty bad shape. They had been physically and mentally abused. They had numerous bruises and were depressed. They cowered at any attention directed at them. It was weeks before they would even look at me. They expected to be abused anytime a man approached them. Months went by before they understood no one was going to hurt them.

"Six months after their arrival, the steamboat made a scheduled stop bringing provisions. I took the girls to the boat, planning to send them down the river to an Asian Embassy in Baghdad. When I directed them to get on the boat, they started crying and pleading with me not to send them away. One of the boat crewmen began talking to them in their native language. They were Vietnamese. The crewman had fought in Vietnam and spoke enough of the language to communicate with them. He explained to them that I was helping them return to Vietnam. The girls told the interpreter they wanted to stay with me. They felt safe and had never been treated so well. They begged me to let them stay. I agreed to their request with the understanding they could leave at any time. A year ago, I again offered to help them return to Vietnam, but they had no desire to return. They have been with me for two years and have learned to speak Arabic. I am very fond of them and would hate to see them leave. Surely, you can see how much I care for them."

***

They ate a meal of wild goat, flatbread, and wine. One of Abdul's bodyguards had gone hunting that morning and killed the goat. Taylor helped him skin and butcher it. After their meal, Abdul offered Taylor a brandy and a cigar. "I see you don't mind blood on your hands."

"I am an avid hunter and have field-dressed a few animals," Taylor said.

Raising his glass of Brandy to Taylor, "Too good hunting and beautiful woman."

"Again, you confound me," Taylor replied.

"Good, you are an evil infidel. I hope to drive you crazy before we part," Abdul said.

does this guy have a sense of humor

"Why do you like the word infidel so much?" Taylor asked.

"What better word to describe a Cherub of Satan," Abdul replied.

Taylor's thoughts were spinning in his head. Most of the questions he had planned to ask were now irrelevant. The personality he had envisioned does not exist. His original assumption of a single-minded, blood-thirsty killer was wrong. Now that he had met and been around Abdul, he began to see a human being, not just a fanatical Islamic terrorist. He found himself wanting to understand him.

I still intend to kill the bastard

Throughout the night, Taylor heard the sound of gunfire in the distance.

The next morning, he was sitting on cushions placed on a large flat rock outside the cave by the girls who were now enamored with him. He was having coffee while waiting for Abdul to join him. He assumed Abdul was in the cave and would come out shortly, but one of Abdul's bodyguards told him that Abdul had left and would be gone for several days.

He was told he was free to explore and photograph the area. But he must be accompanied by the women who will carry a weapon and a satellite phone. He was free to photograph as he pleased but must understand the photos would be checked for anything that might compromise their location. A few minutes later, a vehicle picked up the bodyguard, and they left.

CHAPTER XVII

the terrorist psyche

Taylor gathered his laptop and camera equipment. He told the women, with a few words of Vietnamese they had taught him, that he wanted to go exploring and would like them to come with him.

They walked down a path to the river and along the bank.

A few yards up the river, there was a small cove that made a turn blocking the view so it couldn't be seen from the river. They walked to the back of the cove, where Taylor was shocked to see a US Army patrol boat tied to a wooden dock. Solar panels attached to the dock kept the boat batteries charged and the vessel ready to go at a moment's notice.

He went aboard the boat, and looking under camouflaged tarps, he saw 50-caliber machine guns mounted on the forward and aft decks.

In addition to the boat was a small, fenced pasture with two donkeys that could carry supplies and equipment in an emergency.

Continuing their walk, they found a plateau with a

few trees that could provide shade. Taylor motioned to the women that he wanted to write and would like them to sit a distance away so he could think without being distracted.

After writing for an hour, he closed his laptop and, using his backpack as a pillow, lay back against a large rock to consider several scenarios regarding the best way to kill Abdul.

After a while, he sat up and drank a bottle of water while watching the women. One had lain down on a large flat rock while the other sat beside her. He picked up his camera and started photographing them. He continued taking photos as he walked toward them. The girls looked tired from the heat, so he gestured for them to return to the cave.

It had been two days since Abdul left. He had written for hours each day and felt good about what he had accomplished, considering that he was not a writer by any metric.

He was at his favorite spot outside the cave on a natural stone bench shaded from the sun most of the day. The girls had positioned cushions to provide a comfortable place for him to write.

It was midmorning when the SUV pulled up to the cave. "Get in. I have a good day planned for us," Abdul said.

Taylor grabbed his backpack and got in the SUV. They headed away from the sounds he had heard throughout the night.

After an hour's drive into the mountains, the temperature had dropped considerably.

He remembered his platoon going into the mountains on patrol and how the temperature had changed. There was a firefight and a brother was killed.

They descended into a valley with a small stream flowing through a beautiful meadow of wildflowers in full bloom. The bodyguards opened the rear hatch of the SUV and retrieved fishing equipment.

"Do you know how to fly fish, infidel?"

"What kind of fish are we fishing for?"

"Rainbow and Brown trout."

"Amazing," Taylor said.

They wore waders, rigged their flyrods, walked to the stream, and began fishing.

Abdul spontaneously began talking about his life. "I was born in Kawh, a small village about thirty kilometers from here. A British teacher taught the nine boys in my village to speak English. He would come from Erbil once a week. When I was sixteen, I joined the Mujahideen to fight the Russians after they invaded Afghanistan. The Americans helped us by supplying antiaircraft weapons, and we defeated them.

"I returned to Iraq and joined the army. I got married, but a year into our marriage, my wife and child died while she was giving birth. I became an officer after three years of combat experience in Afghanistan. I have scars to prove it.

"After Saddam Hussein was killed and the Iraqi Army was disbanded, circumstances enabled me to build a small army to protect my village and the surrounding province, what you refer to as a warlord. It is a difficult situation now with the coalition forces occupying my country and so many factions competing for power and land. Sunnis, Shia, Iran, Russia, Syria, Israel, and on and on.

"I try to avoid conflict with the coalition forces, but sometimes we inevitably cross paths and start shooting at one another, too often inflicting casualties before we figure out who is who. It is challenging to encounter coalition soldiers and think of them as friends and enemies simultaneously.

"At first, the West only wanted to ensure a reliable source of oil. Then they got bogged down in geopolitics, and the Middle East blew up in their face. Sadly, as angry as I got with your earlier assessment of my country, much of what you said is true. I am at a loss as to how to bring peace to Iraq.

"I know when American civilians are killed, the response is severe and only worsens the situation. I ask my associates, why do you continue to do this? Ten Iraqis will die for every American civilian you kill. And regarding the airport bombing in the US, my public declaration of taking responsibility for the bombing was a fake statement sent to the news media by another warlord. There is bad blood between us, and he would like the US to kill me so he can take over my province. I have sent numerous messages to the Americans explaining that I had no part in planning or executing the attack, but I don't think they believe me. Maybe you could say something to them."

"Why do factions like yours take credit for attacks

like that?" Taylor asked.

"It is good for recruiting. Different factions compete for the media coverage over who gets to claim a particular attack."

"Do you claim responsibility for attacks you were not involved in?" Taylor asked.

"Regrettably, I have. I didn't think about being credited with attacking civilians because I have never done that," Abdul responded.

"You have never deliberately targeted civilians?" Taylor asked.

"No, I will fight the enemy soldier with all the strength of my body and soul, but I have never intentionally killed a civilian," Abdul proclaimed.

***

Suddenly, everything was upside down. Abdul was not the airport bomber.

The bodyguards cleaned and prepared the fish they caught. After their meal, Abdul produced a bottle of scotch. "You prefer this over the Brandy, yes?"

"It is my choice of whiskey," Taylor replied.

"Let's walk down to the stream and talk," Abdul said as he put the bottle of scotch in a backpack and tossed it over his shoulder.

When they reached the stream, Abdul poured drinks and lit their cigars. "You are corrupting me, infidel. The scotch is very good. I worry that I am spending too much time away from my duties. Tomorrow, I will take you to the village where I grew up. It may help you better understand my country and me."

It wasn't the time to continue their fractious conversation. The atmosphere alluded to a temporary cease-fire in their verbal combat. They returned to a fire made by the bodyguards.

They slept by using the ever-present cushions as a pillow and rain ponchos for cover.

There was little conversation on the drive back to the cave. The silence was comfortable.

CHAPTER XVIII

home village

The bodyguards had the hood up on an old Toyota Landcruiser. It had several whiskey blisters and a thick blanket of dust covering it. The bodyguards had attached a small trailer with a bunch of mannequins secured to the railing and arranged in such a way as to make them look real. Taylor had seen this before and knew what was happening but acted puzzled for Abdul's sake.

"To keep the drone from attacking us," Abdul groused.

"So, I could be killed by a drone that is looking for you," Taylor said.

"Wouldn't that be ironic," Abdul said.

The trip to Abdul's home village was uneventful except for the confrontation with a local village Elder at a crossroads in the middle of nowhere. He claimed Abdul's soldiers had threatened one of his shepherds and were taking too many of his sheep for food. Abdul went to his vehicle, returned with a band of hundred-dollar bills, and gave it to the guy.

Abdul got back in the vehicle, grumbling under his breath. "That old man shakes me down every time we meet."

Entering the walled compound, the place looked deserted. After they stopped in the middle of the village, Abdul motioned for everyone to stay in the vehicle. He got out, walked to the front of the SUV, and stopped. A door opened, and a gray-bearded man came out to meet Abdul. They spoke for quite a while before Abdul waved for everyone to exit the vehicle. He gestured for Taylor to follow him to a door that opened into a single room.

"Rest, I will send for you later, and we will dine and visit with the elders."

Taylor lay down on a rug and used a cushion for a pillow. He fell asleep.

An hour had passed when a bodyguard shook Taylor awake. He splashed bottled water on his face and ran his wet fingers through his hair before following the bodyguard outside.

Rugs and cushions were placed close to a wall that provided shade from the sun. Three village elders were sitting with Abdul.

The two bodyguards carrying their rifles went to the watch tower, where they could view the surrounding area.

Abdul introduced Taylor, explaining why he was with him. The villagers looked at him with disdain. None of them spoke English, so Abdul had to translate their comments.

There were several small villages under Abdul's

control. He treated the residents with respect and was quick to respond with help when it was requested. He was the chief power broker in the region. His temperate command persona belied his fierce conviction to maintain his authority.

The meeting was about how Abdul's soldiers were treating them. Were they respecting the elders, did they have enough food, and were the animals well? Abdul seemed genuinely interested in their well-being.

After the meeting, Abdul told the elders he would tour the village with Taylor.

They walked, and Taylor noted their conversation.

Abdul was reflective while speaking of his childhood and pointing out places he had played. He recounted leaving the village to fight the Russians when they invaded Afghanistan.

Abruptly, Abdul's attitude changed.

"This was a mistake bringing you here. You will find little insight into my psyche by coming here. I was never a child. I was born a warrior. That is all I know, and I am proud of what I have accomplished," he asserted.

Taylor knew not to ask more questions.

Back at the cave, Abdul tells Taylor he and his men must leave again for a day, maybe two.

"The girls will take good care of you," he said with a chuckle. The next morning, after the girls had prepared a meal for him, Taylor explained to them that he was going alone for a walk.

He needed to reevaluate his relationship with

Abdul. Since Abdul explained the events and false credit for the airport bombing, he could not figure out what to do next.

should I pack up and go home
could I actually write a story about this guy

CHAPTER XIX

Taylor is exposed

On his return, there was a dramatic change in Abdul's demeanor. "Come with me," Abdul demanded.

At the knoll where they first met, Abdul again walked dangerously close to the cliff's edge, where falling would surely kill him. He remained silent for an unnerving time before he finally spoke. "Yesterday, as the sun rose, I was praying to Allah when a sudden foreboding came over me. It was the Angel of Death. The Angel told me you were death's messenger, my executioner.

"You deceived me into thinking you wanted to write an article about me so the world might better understand my people and me. I will have you beheaded and left in the desert for the scavengers to peck out your eyes and eat your flesh. If I could think of a more painful death, I would do that to you. You are not just an infidel but a Bastard child of Satan."

"Why are you saying this?" Taylor asked.

"I told you why. Tell me I am wrong," Abdul demanded.

Some way, Abdul had found out the real reason Taylor was there.

He might as well come clean. "After the bombing at the airport in the US that killed so many innocent people, and you took credit for, I swore I would risk everything to kill you. I would be hunting someone else if you had not taken credit for the bombing. My quest to kill you ended when you told me you weren't responsible for the bombing and that you had never intentionally killed civilians. Would you not want to kill me if I had murdered innocent Iraqi civilians? You also promised to return me to Erbil unharmed, no matter the circumstance."

"It is getting cold. I will build a fire," Abdul snarled.

Thinking they were going to the same place to enjoy the view and friendly conversation Taylor had brought a bottle of scotch. He poured them each a drink. "Open your mind for a minute and listen to me," Taylor said, taking a swallow of whiskey.

"A few weeks ago, I was determined to kill the mindless, blood-thirsty bastard that set off the bomb in the US that killed women and children. You could not possibly fathom my hatred for you when we first met. I would have taken great pleasure in cutting off your head and throwing it into a pile of goat shit.

"But then, I find you are not that person. It has been a journey from hatred to respect. Now I want to be the person you thought I was. Given the opportunity, I will write a story with the same determination as I had to kill the terrorist that does not exist in you," Taylor said.

"You had convinced me the US is not as evil as I once thought, but you are more evil than I could ever imagine. You are a lying son-of-a-bitch. You are just trying to save your neck."

Taylor retrieved his camera, showed Abdul how the firearm feature worked, and handed the camera to him. "I've had numerous opportunities to blow your brains out with this. So at least honor my request to shoot me to death. I am betting my life you know what's in my heart."

After a brooding moment, "I will return you to Erbil. I will never trust another American."

"I will not leave until we straighten out this matter," Taylor asserted.

"You are a fool. I am sparing your life," Abdul said.

"The people that falsely credited you for the bombing are the ones you should blame for this situation. I see an opportunity to lessen our fears of one another," Taylor said.

"It is too much. I don't think I could ever trust you again."

Abdul left him.

Taylor walked to the same ledge and precarious place where Abdul had stood.

Now, he genuinely wanted to write a story about Abdul and the Iraqi people more than ever. Everything had changed.

Abdul was not present when he left, but he had a driver return Taylor to Erbil.

CHAPTER XX

Taylor and Kathryn's relationship grows

Taylor took a taxi from the train station to the corporate pilots' lounge at the airport, where Kathryn would pick him up.

Sitting in a chair at a table for the first time in months felt strange after sitting on cushions.

He watched Kathryn taxi the airplane close to the pilot lounge entrance and shut down the engines. Upon entering the lounge, she kissed him, "every day I fully expected to hear that you were dead," she said. As soon as the airplane is fueled, we will head to Cyprus and the closest bar," she laughed.

Upon returning to Cyprus, Ed joined them at their favorite bar and gave Taylor a big bear hug. "Man, it's good to see you in one piece."

They ordered drinks.

Ed was eager to hear about Taylor's adventure.

"Before you talk, I need to debrief Taylor on his operation. Ed, you understand there may be information that should not be discussed. Taylor, come to my office, and we will get this done so we can rejoin Ed and discuss your venture under the security guidelines," she said.

Kathryn had an office in her hotel suite. It was next to a set of double doors that opened to a veranda. She opened the doors to the sounds of the city, and the fragrance of a large jasmine plant growing on the railing filled the room.

"Scotch, right?"

"Yes, thank you."

"The CIA has not determined how Abdul learned of your plan to kill him. I know you have reviewed your conversations with him for one that could have raised his suspicion," she said.

"Yes, I have gone over our conversations and don't remember saying anything that would raise a red flag. I was always mindful of the possibility that my writing and notes might be read. I'm baffled by the turn of events," Taylor said.

Taylor told Kathryn about Abdul not being the perpetrator behind the bombing and how that acknowledgment had completely changed their relationship. Otherwise, he would be dead.

"I envisioned a relationship with Abdul that could benefit both of us before this blowup."

The debriefing took about an hour. "I think we're finished with our business. Come to the veranda, and have another drink before we join Ed."

"I think it is my turn to debrief you," he joked.

"When we first met, you gave me a hard time when I asked about your personal life. Is that still off-limits?"

She seemed eager to answer, "I was born and grew up in California. I had an idyllic childhood. The northern California coast is the perfect place for an adventurous spirit. I probably spent more time in a tent by the ocean or in the mountains than I did in my room at home. Being of Scotch-Irish descent, I'm sure I have Viking blood running through my veins. I joined the Army at twenty. I had an aptitude for tactical operations and worked my way through the system to become an analyst for asymmetric warfare. I did two tours in Iraq and worked closely with the CIA on several operations.

"I left the army after four years of service and went to work for an American defense contractor. I trained military personnel on the weapon systems my company sold them. In the process, I worked with several of the same CIA personnel I had worked with while in the Army.

"The defense contractor job was good, but the more time I spent with the CIA, the more intrigued I became with them and started inquiring about the prospect of joining the organization. Using every contact I had; I was working through the system when a CIA group commander I had known for years contacted me. He heard I was interested in joining the "company" and wanted to talk to me. After meeting with him and other CIA people over the next few weeks, they recommended me for their special operator course."

CHAPTER XXI

flashback

Kathryn becomes a CIA operator

After being recommended for the Special Operations Force (SOF) course, Kathryn was eager to get started and learn the skills required to become an operator. She was flown to a training facility for Special Operator personnel on the east coast of the US.

After checking into the facility, she was on her way to her barrack when she noticed three women instructors practicing a drill routine. They were tossing a rifle, with a bayonet attached to the barrel, in the air from one person to another. She was amazed at their skill. "That looks incredibly dangerous. What are you doing?" she asked.

"We're on the rifle drill team at Fort Bragg," one of the women said. "After our time here as instructors, we will rejoin the team. We work out when we have time. Kathryn watched them until they finished the routine. She applauded them. "That was so cool. Please send me your exhibition schedule. I want to watch you perform."

It was an hour before orientation, so she took the time to walk around the compound and familiarize herself with the location of everything. She noticed several people gathered at a small, aging building off the central plaza. Venturing in, it was the classic bar scene except for alcohol, which was forbidden. It had a warm, welcoming feel. The walls were adorned with framed photos of past classes of graduates and covert operators on the front line of a no-name conflict in the middle of somewhere. People were sitting at the bar or standing in small groups.

She asked the bartender for a glass of tonic water with ice before joining a group standing in front of a fireplace so large a person could walk into it.

People from the US and Israeli intelligence services were there. In addition, ex-military and Private Military Contractor personnel were there, all to prepare for a wide range of vocations.

It was early morning on the first day of the course. The trainees had assembled at a covered pavilion at the obstacle course's starting point. They were chatting and drinking coffee while waiting for their instructors.

Two men and a woman arrived in a Humvee. The driver had long hair and a three-day-old beard. A bald-headed woman wearing black tactical pants and boots, a tan T-shirt, and aviator sunglasses stepped out of the vehicle and addressed the trainees. "Morning folks, my name is Oxie. Welcome to Camp Tranquil. The instructors have been handpicked for their gentle, empathic nature. If you get a scratch or bruise, we will be right there to help you through the pain. So, relax and enjoy the course," she said with a smirk.

"We don't recognize or address anyone by military rank or any other status in this course. You will live and often think you're dying on an equal basis.

She emphasized the rules were the same as the regular Army. "Break one, and you will be kicked out of the program."

***

Four women and twelve men started the course. By week six, two men and two women had dropped out, leaving Kathryn and one other woman the only females. Two more weeks into the program, Kathryn and her friend Becky were holding their own when Becky fractured her wrist and had to drop out.

After a grueling day of obstacle course work, the group was allowed to build a fire on the beach, eat some MREs, and sleep until dawn, a few hours away.

Out of nowhere, a bottle of whiskey appeared and was passed around. Kathryn said no at first but gave in after being ragged by the guys, "Macallan, you're a wimp, let's see some bitch."

The last woman in the class, she was determined to hold her own with this testosterone-fueled band of masculinity.

when the bad guys show up, and the shit hits the fan, these are the people I want on my six

She took a sip from the bottle. The evening

progressed, and everyone was getting intoxicated to one degree or another when someone commented that it was time for the ritual of branding the new trainees with the Jolly Roger Flag. The ritual started when someone took a skull and crossbones insignia and filed sharp points on it. Dipped in tattoo ink, the insignia would be pressed into the chest hard enough to puncture the skin, leaving a permanent imprint that would be recognized by the spec-op brotherhood.

The group had become close friends, and the guys didn't think Kathryn should participate. They were discussing the issue when it was suggested that if she was determined to participate in the ritual, have the flag put on her butt.

After the rite, everyone joked about branding Kathryn on the butt. "When you're walking down the beach in a bikini with the Jolly Roger flying on your ass, any operator will know who you are," one of the guys jested.

Continuing to pass the whiskey around, the guys talked Kathryn into trying a pinch of smokeless tobacco with the whiskey. They explained how to keep the two separated in her mouth and not swallow the tobacco with the whiskey.

But, even doing it half-ass right, the rush of nicotine into her blood mixed with too much whiskey made her retching sick.

It was a few minutes before daylight when the instructors showed up. Kathryn had passed out and was so sick she couldn't stand. Her hair was matted with vomit and sand. One of the guys had placed a towel under her head to keep her face out of the sand.

The instructors sitting in the Humvee didn't notice her condition when they instructed everyone to go to the water. "Line up parallel to the surf, sit down, and lock arms at a point where the waves will hit you in the face; let's go," he ordered. Her colleagues dragged her to the beach out of sight of the instructors. They locked arms as instructed and sat facing the surf. The freezing cold waves crashed into their bodies, completely submerging them. The water splashing in her face actually helped a bit.

Trembling uncontrollably, they endured the constant soaking until the instructors determined they were near hypothermia. At the instructors' direction, they crawled far enough from the surf to escape the waves and huddled together to generate what heat was left in their bodies.

Daylight revealed a cold, exhausted, sleep-deprived pile of bodies. "Damn good job y'all. That exercise usually eliminates two or three folks, but y'all hung in there, congrats," an instructor said.

"I will reward you with an easy five-mile run through the dunes, a mile swim across the bay, and finish the day on the firing range. Let's go," the instructor ordered.

The guys helped Kathryn stand but had no choice but to leave her and start running down the beach. She tried to run but fell within a few yards. She tried to stand again but dropped to her knees, then lay down. The head instructor saw her lying on the ground. "Macallan, what is your problem, are you hurt?" he asked.

"I'm sick," she mumbled.

Turning to the other two instructors, "Put her in your vehicle and take her to sick bay."

As they loaded her into the vehicle, "She's reeking of alcohol; she's drunk," an instructor said.

"Where did the alcohol come from? Who else was drinking?" he asked Kathryn. After a long drunken pause, "Some locals having a party came by in a boat and offered me a drink. I made a terrible decision. I'm sorry."

"You were the only one that drank alcohol with the civilians?"

"Yes," she replied.

"I'll say you made a bad decision; it was stressed at orientation that alcohol was forbidden. Damn it, Macallan, I was rooting for you. I saw the determination to complete this program and join that elite group of special operators. Then you blow it with this stupid ass stunt. You're done. Get the hell out of my sight."

Kathryn finished stuffing the last personal item into her duffel bag.

The door of the base transit bus closed off all that she had worked so hard for and had let so many people down. Returning to Cyprus and her old job, a failure, was almost too much to endure. Still, she had decided that she would do whatever it took to reclaim her standing.

A week had passed. Kathryn was in her office mindlessly shuffling paperwork to keep from screaming at her stupidity when she received a text to meet her boss in the command center of the embassy.

En route to the command center conference room, every possible thought of what she might say was, in the end, just bullshit.

you have no one to blame but yourself for what's coming
look the boss in the eye and take whatever he says
Take it like the pain in the ass of being branded
show him the flag on my ass

She entered the command center operations room expecting her boss to be the only one there, but the course instructors and some people she trained with were there. She was puzzled to see them. "I know you are in pain and confused, so let me explain. Everything that occurred in the training course was choreographed right down to the alcohol. We emphasize the physical part of the course, which is demanding and eliminates a lot of people. But psychological aptitude is just as critical for the work you are about to commence.

"Due to your stalwart actions to protect your teammates from failing the course for drinking alcohol with you and how you conducted yourself in a disconcerting and stressful situation, the company would like to welcome you into the Special Operators Group. Congratulations," the Boss said.
"I'll be damn," she thought.

end flashback

CHAPTER XXII

Taylor and Kathryn's relationship grows

"Well, that's my story, four years in the Army and six years with the CIA. I love what I do and would not trade jobs with anyone."

"Wow, you have covered a lot of ground in your career. I assume you're not married. What about kids or boyfriends?" he asked.

"Never married, no kids. I've had a couple of beaux, but my work is not conducive to a relationship. I live in this hotel most of the time because I travel so much. I visit family two or three times a year."

"Enough about me. Same questions for you?" she asked.

"You know my military background and like you, I spent most of my time outdoors. I love to hunt and fish.

"My wife died in a plane crash four years ago. Since then, I have had a few dates but should have gone fishing instead."

Tentative for a moment, she downed the last of her drink and kissed him. "Take me to a nice restaurant this evening, then stay with me tonight," she brazenly proposed.

Stunned, he tossed down the last of his drink. "I'll call Ed and tell him the debriefing is going to take much longer than we first thought and not to wait," he joked.

On returning to Kathryn's hotel suite after a pleasant dinner, she was making drinks when there was a knock on the door, "room service."

"There must be a mistake," she said. When she opened the door, a bellhop was there with a massage table. "Good evening Ms. Macallan. Where would you like the table placed?"

She looked at Taylor, "I'm impressed."

She showered and lay on the table in her darkened bedroom.

After a thorough massage with a lotion the concierge had recommended, he placed warm flat stones on her back. After a few minutes, he removed the stones and dripped ice water down her spine with a sponge.

She moaned.

"You sound like my Labrador Retriever, Sally when I rub her back with my feet," he laughed.

"Lawton, you say the most romantic things."

The next morning, they walked to Kathryn's favorite restaurant for breakfast. The ambiance of the outside setting overlooking the ocean complimented their new relationship.

"I have the time. Would you like to rent a car and drive along the coast? We could take a basket of food.

There are several scenic places to stop," she said.

Walking on an isolated and beautiful stretch of beach with Kathryn, this circumstance had never entered his mind when planning this venture.

The last rays of sunlight were dancing on the water, "Is it the ocean, or you, that makes this wine taste so good?" she said as they walked on the white sand beach and in the surf up to their ankles.

He grabbed her hand and pulled her deeper into the surf, "The quantity is most likely the culprit," he jested.

"Bud, that will cost you," she bantered as she splashed water on him.

CHAPTER XXIII

renew relationship with warlord

Taylor and Ed had been back in Cyprus for six weeks. They had driven and sailed around the island extensively.

They were contemplating returning to the US when he received a text from Kathryn. "We need to talk. I have news."

It had been weeks since he last saw her. They met for drinks at their favorite restaurant and planned the evening together.

"It has been a while. Is another guy buying you better wine?" he asked. "I'm currently involved in an operation and could be adding a second. Abdul wants to meet with you. He gave no reason.

"I'm looking forward to our evening, but as usual, I have work to do," she said.

"When would be a good time for you to meet at Ed's boat?" he asked. "To finish work and transform into Cinderella, I would say seven. Is that okay?"

"That works for me," he said.

When Kathryn arrived at the boat, Taylor was the

only one there. "Where's Ed?"

"I paid him to get lost," he grinned.

"I don't know about being alone with a sailor and a bottle of wine," she said.

Not being the sailor Ed was, and there being little wind to sail, Taylor used the diesel engine to motor up the coast.

The lights from the city reflecting off the water created a quixotic atmosphere. She went below and made drinks.

Returning to the topside, she handed Taylor his drink. "Thank you," he said.

"Do you ever take a vacation"? he asked.

"I thought I needed that a few years back and took a few weeks off. I had never been to Australia's Great Barrier Reef, so I rented a place on the beach. I met a bunch of crazy Aussies at a nearby marina and was soon invited to go sailing and nonstop partying. I did the whole vacation thing, in addition to adding a couple of pounds to my ass. I had a wonderful time. Then I woke up on day six or seven thinking, okay, that was fun, but I'm on the next flight out of here. I love what I do and couldn't wait to return to work. Isn't that crazy?"

They entered a small bay where several boats were anchored and found a good spot where they were the proper distance from a neighboring boat and the beach.

"After anchoring the boat, Taylor lowered the dinghy into the water and motored them to the beach.

Papa Jack's restaurant was a favorite of the sailing

fraternity. It had been added to over the years, with each addition adding to its eclectic décor. Right on the water, the restaurant was just a few yards from where the dinghy landed on the beach.

The dance floor was a wooden deck with lights strung from corner to corner. There was a raised platform for a band and a bar at one end. They had a pleasant dinner and danced. They walked on the beach for a while before returning to the boat. Taylor poured her a glass of white wine and himself a scotch.

"You did good, Mr. Taylor," as she clinked his glass.

"Do I get a reward?" he asked.

"Maybe. Did you bring my favorite massage lotion?" she asked.

When Taylor woke the next morning, Kathryn was already topside, sitting comfortably on some cushions, drinking coffee.

He joined her with a carafe of coffee. "Good morning, early bird," he said as he poured her a fresh cup and one for himself.

"This is the perfect time of day to be on the water," she beamed.

"Even more so for me, because a beautiful woman is in the picture," he said.

"Lawton, you're full of it," she said

They went ashore for breakfast and strolled on the beach, letting the waves wash over their feet. They walked a considerable distance looking for unusual shells that may have washed up on the beach. They put a handful of the most colorful and unique ones in Taylor's backpack.

After swimming, they sat on a blanket and had mimosas.

"You're spoiling me," she sighed.

Returning to the sailboat, they motored back to the marina.

"I have made arrangements to fly you back to Erbil. You will be picked up at the train station by the same guy that picked you up before," she said.

"I think we should sail off to Australia, lie on the beach in the shade of a palm tree, drink gin and tonics, and do other good stuff. That sounds much better than hanging out with a bunch of crazy Arabs. But yeah, I know, maybe someday down the road, but right now, get your ass in gear and get back to work," he said.

"I'll put that trip on my calendar," she said.

CHAPTER XXIV

make amends

The same guy picked him up in Erbil. He was less hostile than when they first met. They took the same route as the first time for an hour or so before the driver changed direction. After driving for another hour in the new direction, they came over a rise to see Abdul's Mercedes parked in the shade of a cliff wall. Taylor's driver let him out and drove away a distance, joining Abdul's bodyguards.

He was uneasy about their meeting, considering their troubled parting. Abdul was alone, leaning on the hood of his Mercedes, wearing a shoulder holster with a pistol.

The ever-present rugs and cushions were arranged on the ground in the shade of a cliff wall.

Abdul opened the rear hatch of his SUV and retrieved a bottle of scotch. He poured two drinks and handed one to Taylor. "Thanks," Taylor said.

After a moment of looking Taylor in the eye, "I have resolved my anger with you by admitting to myself that I was wrong reacting the way I did when it was disclosed to me your original intention of coming here. And I know you could have sent soldiers or a drone to kill me. That tells me you were truthful in your change of heart after realizing I was not the person you sought.

"The reason you came to Iraq was to kill the person that planned the attack that killed women and children in a terrorist bombing in your country. And you came after me because you thought I was the one who planned and executed the attack. I was angry enough to kill you for deceiving me, but I was wrong. As you said, I would have done the same thing if the situation had been reversed.

The conversation was initially uncomfortable, but they slowly broke the ice of suspicion. Both spoke in a conciliatory manner, wanting to repair their relationship.

"I have thought about how we might work together if you are willing to set aside this fractious incident. I would like you to consider collaborating with me as a liaison to the coalition forces. Also, I would like to develop and support a covert operator relationship with you. I will not work with the US directly. It is difficult enough to justify working with one infidel," Abdul said, with a smirk on his face regarding the use of the word that had become an expression of friendly banter before their relationship had blown up.

"I'm listening," Taylor responded.

"I will help you kill the person who planned the attack on your country. His name is Rahid Beqham. I have never respected him because of his blood lust. He is a cold, cruel man who has gained enough power to reject our relationship. He is pursuing an agenda that directly conflicts with what I have worked so hard to build.

"If I send my soldiers against him, blood will be spilled, and I want to avoid that. A drone strike that kills just Rahid and his bodyguards would be an ideal scenario, and I know the US is particularly good at that.

"I have worked with American covert operators and have seen their value firsthand. I would like to build that type of relationship with you. I see the benefit of an operator that will allow me to distance my organization from political issues. It would also give me more flexibility in my future plans," Abdul said.

"I must return to Erbil or Cyprus to discuss this with my people. How do I get back to you?" Taylor asked.

"How much time do you need?" Abdul asked. "I would guess a week," Taylor said.

"The driver will take you back and wait for you to call him."

The trip back to Erbil seemed to take forever and was unusually tiring. He was exhausted when the driver let him off at the train station. There was a hotel across the street. He got a room and crashed onto the bed.

The following day, he contacted Kathryn. "I need to talk with you as soon as possible."

She understood they should not discuss the matter over the phone. "I will make arrangements to fly you to Cyprus. I will meet you there in two days."

They met at their favorite restaurant, had a light lunch, then went to her hotel suite. She made drinks, and they sat on the veranda.

Taylor told her of Abdul's offer. "Wow, what a change, but I appreciate his position. He has realized that you are the key to eliminating Rahid and wants to rebuild the relationship. It also sounds like he has come to recognize the value of the covert operator. And that you are the only one he would consider working with in that capacity. Our intel all along thought Rahid was involved in the airport attack, and this confirms it. But when Abdul took credit for the attack, we took him at his word," she said.

CHAPTER XXV

abducted

Taylor got the impression the driver liked him more each time they made a trip together. He even knew his name now. "Hey, Efren, how are you?" Taylor asked as he threw his gear into the bed of the truck. Efren smiled at Taylor, saying his name, and waved at him.

An hour into the trip, Taylor pulled his baseball cap down over his eyes to rest for a few minutes but fell asleep. Thirty minutes had passed when he was awakened by the sound of voices. The truck had stopped, and Efren, the driver, was gone.

Two guys were standing in front of a truck, holding AK-47 rifles. Taylor pulled his pistol from inside his jacket and held it below the door window so it couldn't be seen from the outside. One of the guys walked toward his truck and motioned for him to get out.

Taylor's mind was spinning. All he could think to say was, "Abdul-Hadi, Abdul-Hadi."

The guy yelled for Taylor to get out of the truck and shouldered his rifle as if he were going to shoot him if he didn't obey the command. It had been years since he was in combat, but the adrenaline made it yesterday.

"Okay," Taylor said.

In one continuous motion, he opened the truck door, did a forward roll to the ground as if he had tripped, and fired three rounds into the guy's chest. In another split second, he put three rounds into the other guy before he could react to Taylor's sudden move.

It would take too long to set up a satellite feed to figure out his location and the direction he needed to go, so he used a standard compass to determine the direction of North. Knowing the sound of a weapon firing carried a great distance in the open desert, he quickly left the place in his truck. He took the faint road in the desert sand that headed in the general direction he thought would take him to Abdul's camp.

It was getting dark when he made it to the foothills. He found a place off the road where he couldn't be seen and set up camp for the night. He had an MRE meal before putting everything back in the truck except his sleeping bag in case he needed to leave quickly. He settled in for the night. Lying in his sleeping bag, he had time to reflect on the day's events.

It was first light when the crack of rifle fire and a bullet careening off a large bolder inches from his face jolted him awake. He grabbed his weapon and looked to see two trucks, five guys, and a German Shepherd about a hundred yards from him. The men were behind the trucks with their rifles pointed at him. There was no practical way to escape from his position. One of the guys held up an RPG launcher to convince him to surrender.

He raised his arms. While one guy with a rifle held it on him, another tied his hands and blindfolded him.

He was pushed into his vehicle. One guy drove while another sat in the truck's bed with his rifle pointed at him through the back window.

They drove for what seemed like hours before the vehicle stopped. Taylor was removed from the vehicle and pushed, still blindfolded, into a building. He could hear the squeaking sound of door hinges. He was pushed into a small room so hard he almost fell. There was metal-to-metal clanging, then silence. After standing in one spot for so long, he slowly lay on the floor.

Hours passed, and his back was killing him. He was miserable. Finally, two guards entered the room, removed the blindfold, and untied his hands while the other guard held a rifle on him. He was in a prison cell with four empty walls. The guards didn't say a word before leaving. Exhausted, he moved to a corner of the cell, lay down, and fell asleep.

He was awakened by the sound of metal clanging. A guard had pushed a metal bowl of broth and a saucer with a piece of bread through a small gap in the bars at the floor.

After days in the cell with no windows, he lost track of time. A tiny gap in the wood planks covered the only window. He could tell day from night. The only other light came from a single dim lightbulb down the hall. There was barely enough light to see inside his cell. No one spoke to him. There was dead silence except for the guard bringing him food and the sound of rats scurrying across the floor. He could feel his mental state declining into despair and depression. Each day he kept thinking someone would come and talk to him, but no one came. He also worried that he would be tortured at any time.

Curled up on half of a blanket with the other half pulled over him for warmth, he slept on the floor in the corner of his cell.

Weeks passed when he was awakened by two guards entering his cell. They gestured for him to stand. His hands were tied behind his back before being led outside a courtyard. The first thing Taylor saw was a hanging gallows with three ropes swaying in the air. The guards left him.

An hour passed before three men came from a building across the courtyard and approached Taylor. With a composed demeanor, one of the men wearing dark sunglasses commented to him, "I would like to know a little about you before you are hanged. It is not important. I just thought it might be of interest." Taylor could only think of the same thing he said to the guys he shot. "I'm a journalist. I'm working with Abdul-Hadi. Contact him, and he will straighten this out. I am under his protection."

"Abdul's protection is not working so well for you, is it? Hang him," the guy growled to the guards. The noose was pulled over his head and tightened around his neck. At this moment of imminent death, Taylor

123

steeled himself to show no emotion.

After an agonizing time waiting for that last instant of mortality, the noose was removed.

"I am impressed with your character. For that strength, I will stay your execution for another day. We will play a game to determine the day the noose snaps your American neck. Once a week, you will be brought to the courtyard and have the noose put around your neck. You will throw a pair of dice. The day you throw snake eyes, you will be hanged," he said.

He was returned to his cell and roughly forced into it. He was emotionally drained. He screamed to relieve the tension.

CHAPTER XXVI

rescued

Something was wrong. Abdul had sent a driver to pick up Taylor weeks ago. He kept thinking he would show up any day. He dispatched two of his men to go to several villages to see if anyone knew anything about an American in the area. They came back with no information about Taylor. He had vanished. Abdul sent a message to Shilam al Bekhamn, who set up the interview for Taylor. He knew nothing about him.

Kathryn's first thought.

he's dead

She contacted the CIA for any information or media chatter about an American being captured in that time frame. They had not heard anything and had not received any data. The situation looked hopeless, with no way to coordinate in real-time with Abdul.

Breaking all the rules, Kathryn contacted Ed and asked him to meet her.

At her apartment, she informed Ed of the situation. "What about the guy that picked Taylor up. Do we know anything about him?" Ed asked.

"We know he doesn't live in Erbil. He comes into town on Highway 16. He never stops for anything but goes straight to the train station to pick Taylor up," she answered.

I wonder if there are surveillance cameras at the train station?" Ed asked.

Getting the video from the train station security cameras took two days. Kathryn loaded the video onto her laptop. She and Ed watched intently the segment showing Taylor getting into the driver's truck. They were hoping to see the vehicle's license plate. Finally, the camera captured the plate as the vehicle left the station. Kathryn had her people run a check on the plate. The data showed that the license plate belonged to a vehicle reported stolen over a year ago.

"Well, that was a waste of time. Let's take a break, go for a walk, and get some fresh air," Ed fumed.

They walked for quite a while before stopping at a restaurant with outside tables. They ordered iced tea, small-talked, and people watched for a time to clear their minds.

Why was he going back? Ed asked.

She hesitated before answering him.

"What I'm about to tell you is classified."

She told Ed everything she knew about the operation.

"So, this Abdul guy was going to help Taylor kill the guy that actually planned the airport attack in the US."

"Yes, that was the plan," she responded.

"And he was carrying a tracking device you had

given him, and with the help of this Abdul guy, they planned to put it on the warlord's vehicle?" Ed asked.

Kathryn shrieked, "Damn it, Ed, that's it. Why didn't I think of that?"

It was late. There were few people in the CIA operations center. Someone with the necessary authorization had to be called. It took almost an hour before that person could get there. It took another few minutes for the technician to set up the satellite to search for the tracking device. Kathryn grabbed her laptop. She had access to the satellite computer used to track the device. "I hope the device is still near him and no one has discovered it," she said. The satellite was in search mode. "Come on, come on, please," she begged. And there it was, Taylor's location, or at least the device's location. Kathryn contacted the CIA group over Taylor's operation. She sent them a snapshot of a small map section with a pin that would have no significance to anyone except the CIA and Abdul. The CIA unit commander dispatched a courier to Shilam with the data. It took two days to get the data to Abdul.

The tracking device was on an island thirty miles upriver from Abdul's camp.

Abdul assembled his crew of men trained to operate the patrol boat. Prepared for the operation, they headed up the river.

Abdul knew from the map and pin precisely where to go because the village they were heading to was jointly controlled by Rahid and him.

It was getting dark when they stopped for the night

on the sandy bank of the river. Abdul and his men set up camp and built a small fire.

After a simple dinner, they smoked the hookah and formulated a plan of action in case Rahid was in the village.

"Why are you putting so much effort into rescuing this American?" one of his soldiers asked.

"I understand your misgivings. He came to kill me, but now we're collaborating. I will tell you that I have found him to embody the warrior spirit throughout the time I have known him. Where most fear and avoid risk, he embraces it. He came here with revenge and hate in his heart. But now that he has lived among us, I believe he has a much better understanding of the Iraqi people. Is he a soldier of fortune, a mercenary? I don't think so.

"I believe he is committed to helping Iraq become self-reliant. He acknowledges Islam as the religion of our culture and has no desire to change it. We were working on a more official relationship when Rahid captured him. When we reach the village tomorrow, I ask that you consider him an ally and fight for him if necessary."

The village was on the border of Rahid and Abdul's provinces. It was used as a neutral meeting place to discuss commerce and other issues that arose from time to time. It was the perfect place to hold Taylor. It was the last place Abdul would have thought of when looking for him.

A herd of sheep was spotted a few miles from the island village. They stopped the boat, and Abdul talked with the shepherd. In casual conversation, he got the latest news and generally what was happening in the village and surrounding area. The shepherd knew about Taylor. He told Abdul that Rahid had been in the village a few days earlier but had left with his men. Abdul felt relieved when the shepherd told him Rahid and his soldiers were not in the village. He would not have to battle Rahid's soldiers and get people killed.

The boat pulled up to the village dock. Abdul left the boat and walked up a worn path to meet the village elder waiting for him in the shade of a tree. They exchanged pleasantries, smoked the hookah, and discussed concerns about the village's food supply and safety.

After visiting for an hour, Abdul went to the boat and returned to the Elder with two bundles of US hundred-dollar bills. After walking through the village and visiting with everyone, Abdul told the Elder he was there to pick up the American. He did not elaborate but gave the impression that he had ordered the American's capture.

He knew, without asking, that Rahid was the culprit and was holding him for ransom. Otherwise, he would have killed him. The Elder did not question him.

He told his men to blindfold and tie Taylor's hands before they took him from his cell and to take him directly to the boat. He also instructed his men to not speak to Taylor. Abdul did not want him to react to his release in a manner that could confuse the Elder.

While the men were doing as instructed, two villagers loaded Taylor's personal effects onto the boat.

With Taylor safely on board, they headed back to Abdul's camp. There was total silence for fifteen minutes before Abdul instructed the boat captain to slow the boat and for a crewman to untie his hands. "Remove the blindfold infidel." Bewildered, Taylor removed the blindfold. "What is the American expression? You look like shit."

"I can't decide whether to hug or cuss you," Taylor stammered.

"I will try to explain everything after we return to camp. You are safe now," Abdul said.

But, no sooner had Abdul spoken when rifle fire burst from two trucks full of soldiers racing down the riverbank.

Rahid had returned to the village, and finding Taylor had been released, he was trying to intercept and recover him. Abdul yelled for the captain to take off and for crew members to man the machine guns on each end of the boat, but one crewman was hit before he could move to the weapon.

Taylor had often operated a 50-caliber "ma-duce" machine gun in the Army. He jumped behind the mounted weapon, jacked a bullet into the chamber with the charging handle, and with the help of the crewman on the rear gun, destroyed the trucks and killed several enemy soldiers.

The machine guns were still smoking from the rapid firing when Taylor remarked, "The old adage, "don't bring a knife to a gunfight," applies to this fight. Don't bring an infantry rifle to fight a 50-caliber machine gun. You will lose that battle." Taylor swore.

The river had too many obstacles to navigate at night, and they needed to care for the injured crewman. They motored the boat onto a sandy bank and tied it to a tree. Abdul had not planned to spend the night on the river, so there was no camping equipment. They would have to sleep on the boat cushions as best they could. There were boxes of MREs, so they had plenty to eat. After the starvation rations he had been on in prison, the MREs tasted like he was in a five-star restaurant. He had lost ten pounds during his captivity.

It was close to noon when they got back to camp. The girls had prepared a meal. They were happy to see Taylor and hugged him like an old friend. Taylor ate like it was his last meal. Then, he went to his place in the cave and crashed.

It was late morning when he awakened, showered, and wore fresh clothes.

Abdul was waiting for him in the tent. "After breakfast, we will go to the knoll, and I will explain what happened."

At the knoll, Abdul recalled Taylor's ordeal with Rahid.

"At some point, Efren, the driver must have told one of Rahid's men about you, intentionally or innocently. Rahid planned to ransom you for money."

Taylor told Abdul about the mental torture he endured and didn't know it was Rahid who captured him.

CHAPTER XXVII

attempt to kill an opposing warlord

"Rahid has lost his purpose, and his quest for power has blinded him. His indiscriminate killing has gone too far, and abducting you was the last straw."

Abdul knew the people in the provincial village who were sympathetic to him and those supporting Rahid. Abdul sent two of his most loyal men back to the village where Taylor had been imprisoned.

Rahid's military headquarters camp was a few miles from the provincial village.

Abdul's men were from the village, so there was no concern about their presence, and they blended into daily life. This was an everyday occurrence. They were there for some R&R and to visit family and friends.

A week passed before Rahid came to the village. When they got the chance one night, they planted the tracking device on Rahid's vehicle. The next day, Abdul had them picked up.

Taylor and Abdul were talking about hunting wild goats and trout fishing. They both wanted to return to the relationship they had before their rift.

"The device has been placed on Rahid's vehicle," Abdul said.

Taylor turned on the laptop Kathryn had given him, entered the password, and waited for a satellite connection. Once the satellite made the connection, he requested it to find the tracking device. Within a few seconds, an icon started blinking on the laptop map showing the device's location in the village.

Taylor presented the data to Abdul and got the impression that the reality of what was about to happen was making Abdul have second thoughts about killing Rahid.

"I have known Rahid since childhood. I would never have imagined this situation," Abdul said.

Abdul became more human whenever they talked about their respective lives, politics, and religion.

Taylor was also having difficulty suppressing the hatred he had for Rahid. The mental torture he had put him through by telling him he would be hanged any day was hard to dismiss. But he forced himself to focus on executing the plan as a straightforward military operation.

On the second day after the device had been placed on Rahid's vehicle, the drone control center notified Taylor that Rahid's vehicle was moving. Taylor accessed the map on his computer and could see the icon moving. When the drone controller linked up with the satellite and locked on the tracking device, the weapon system was activated so the controller could select the proper ordnance for this particular type of target.

When the vehicle reached a predetermined point in an isolated area away from the village, where there would be no collateral damage, the controller fired a missile from the drone. The computer icon started blinking and changing color, indicating the vehicle had been destroyed.

There was confused emotion on Abdul's face.

"I am a terrible person. Allah will punish me for this."

It was difficult for Abdul to speak rationally about his feelings regarding Rahid's death.

"I will go to Rahid's people and reassure them that I will care for them. His lieutenants may challenge me about who should replace him. I hope to avoid more bloodshed."

When Taylor got up the following morning and came out of the cave, Abdul was in his tent drinking tea.

"I must go to Rahid's funeral and act quickly to secure the loyalty of his people."

Abdul prepared to leave for the village.

"I don't know how long I will be gone. Stay if you wish or go back to Erbil."

"I will wait for your return," Taylor replied.

Taylor sent Kathryn an encrypted message about the drone strike and Abdul's plans.

"I believe I have convinced Abdul that the coalition forces have no desire to occupy Iraq and will leave as soon as Al-Radea is defeated, and the Iraqi Army is strong enough to defend the country."

"That he was instrumental in killing Rahid

suggests you may be right," Kathryn said.

"He has been adamant about not working directly with the coalition forces. So, the best relationship may be to continue the one we have now, but with a more strategic liaison with the coalition forces so they can concentrate more on Al-Radea," Taylor said.

He reiterated his conversation with Kathryn to Abdul.

"This is happening so fast. I feel like I'm conspiring with the enemy. I am working with people who yesterday were trying to kill me. I am surely insane. I will honor this relationship, but I will not betray my people. I won't be a puppet to the US," Abdul said.

He beckoned for the girls to bring food and coffee.

They ate and continued discussing the event and the structure of their future relationship.

CHAPTER XXVIII

Ambushed

Abdul left for the funeral.

Taylor never thought of the girls as prostitutes and always treated them respectfully. They had become good friends and photography subjects. They were comfortable with Taylor photographing them now and enthusiastically embraced whatever he asked.

*****

Abdul had been gone three days. Taylor was at his favorite place typing on his laptop when Abdul's SUV came speeding up to the cave. A bodyguard exited the vehicle yelling for Taylor to help as he opened the rear of the SUV. Abdul was lying on his side with blood covering his pants. There was fear and pain on his face.

"Rahid is not dead. He was waiting to ambush us," the bodyguard said.

Taylor grabbed Abdul's arm and, with the bodyguard's help, carried him to the tent and laid him down. He yelled for the girls to bring a first aid kit. Taylor used a pair of scissors to cut Abdul's pant leg open. He had a bullet wound in his left hip. Taylor sterilized and sutured the wound to stop the bleeding. Next, he applied a packet of iodine and placed a trauma patch on the wound.

The girls bathed him as best they could. "I must kill Rahid before he tries to take over my province."

"Are there weapons here?" Taylor asked. Abdul told his bodyguards to take Taylor to his store of weapons. A bodyguard gestured for Taylor to follow him.

They went to a part of the cave that Taylor didn't know existed. There were crates of firearms and ammunition. Taylor selected a familiar M24 sniper rifle, an M4 rifle, a 45-caliber pistol, ammunition, and cases of MREs (Meals Ready to Eat).

All the while he was preparing to leave, he was trying to decide what to do next. Finally, he piled everything he was taking outside the cave entrance.

Abdul kept two donkeys for situations like this. He loaded everything onto one donkey except the pistol he would carry in a shoulder holster. Taylor's Army unit had used donkeys in this manner.

"Take Abdul and the girls to your safest village and have a doctor care for him," Taylor said to the bodyguards.

He gave Abdul a painkiller and, with the help of the bodyguards, laid him on some cushions to make him comfortable.

"You confound me, infidel."

"Hey, that's my line," Taylor replied.

He hugged the girls. The next minute he was alone. He watched the SUV disappear into the distance.

CHAPTER XXIX

the hunter

Taylor scratched the donkey behind his ears. "What am I going to call you, my friend? How about Sue, even though you're a Jack. I would have preferred your girlfriend Jenny, but it looks like you've knocked her up, so don't give me any bullshit, or should I say donkey shit," Taylor joked.

With bridle in hand, Taylor started on his original quest to kill the terrorist that bombed the airport in the US but with even more passion.

After hours of walking, it was getting dark. He found a spot with an unobstructed view of the surrounding area so he could see anything approaching from a distance. He unloaded the packs Sue was carrying and tied the end of the bridle to a large stone so he wouldn't stray too far but could drag it around to graze on the sparse vegetation.

"I'm glad you came along so we can talk politics. Obviously, you're a Democrat," Taylor said with a chuckle.

He sent an encrypted message to Kathryn

explaining what had happened. She responded that she would start working on a plan to support him.

Afraid he might be seen he didn't build a fire but had a hot meal using an MRE heater. He had a lot to think about, but he was exhausted. He got in his sleeping bag and fell asleep.

It was barely daylight when he woke. Waiting a few minutes, he decided there was enough light that a small fire couldn't be seen from a distance. After an MRE breakfast and coffee, he formulated a plan to kill Rahid. He messaged Kathryn again, updating her on his situation and receiving the latest information on Rahid.

She had worked through the night to acquire as much data as possible about Rahid.

"I see your location via satellite. You are forty-three miles east of the village where you were imprisoned. Rahid's main military base is four miles north of the village.

"We supported Rahid in the past, so we are familiar with his operation. We don't know why he has turned against us, but we do believe if he is eliminated, Abdul would be even more inclined to work with us." Kathryn said.

"I'm all in on eliminating Rahid, but another attempt with a drone strike is unlikely now. I think a sniper shot is the best alternative. I'm trying to recall the landscape around the village from my time there. I remember a hill overlooking the compound and a line of trees growing against the outside wall on the other side, away from the hill. I have a sniper rifle that I am proficient with from my Army days. I'm confident I can kill the S-O-B with it, given the opportunity," Taylor said.

"I will have a satellite zero in on the village and surrounding area to provide a detailed topographic map. I'm also working on picking you up by helicopter as soon as possible after you kill Rahid. We need to know if it will be possible to extract you from where you take the shot or if you will have to move to a different location. The timing will be critical. Rahid's people will know where the shot came from and will come after you," Kathryn responded.

Taylor closed the conversation, loaded up, and headed for the village. He looked at his laptop linked to the satellite for GPS directions every hour.

He walked a ridge line as much as possible to avoid being caught in the open desert. He figured walking eight hours a day with a couple of breaks, he should reach his destination in four or five days.

It was day two. He had been walking for three hours when he stopped to give Sue and himself a break. He unloaded the packs strapped to Sue so he could cool off and gave him water.

While they rested, he scanned their route to the village with his binoculars. He was high enough to see a good two miles distance in the flat desert landscape. He didn't want to accidentally run into an enemy.

Not expecting to see anything, he was startled when he saw several vehicles and a helicopter about a half mile from him. They were parked in a large semicircle. He determined the vehicles were US equipment. Stryker's, MRAPS, and Humvees bristled with every weapon system in the US arsenal.

He observed a vehicle approaching the camp. As it turned into the camp, he saw a skull with its top blown off, painted on the protective shield of a thirty-millimeter chain gun mounted on a Stryker vehicle. Continuing to glass the area, he saw several soldiers building a wooden structure.

He messaged Kathryn giving her the coordinates to the camp, and asked if she would inquire about what was happening.

It was two hours before she responded. "I pissed off a bunch of people by simply asking about the coordinates you sent me. At first, I thought you had stumbled into a combat operation. But what is actually happening is the boss, a Lieutenant Colonel, is flying in some unauthorized entertainment for his guys after an extremely dangerous operation that put the hurt on a troupe of bad guys. The operation will probably hit the news in a few days.

If you would like, I will see if I can get you an invite. You could use a little R&R. Think about it and let me know," she said.

CHAPTER XXX

R&R

After receiving the okay to join the event, Taylor loaded up Sue and started walking toward the camp.

The site was located on a plateau, making it difficult for an enemy to approach undetected and easy for a helicopter to land.

The perimeter of the camp was heavily guarded. The soldiers on duty had been told about Taylor, so they wouldn't shoot him when they saw him approaching the camp.

He was welcomed into the camp by a slap on the back and a beer in his hand. The guys had been around enough covert operators to presume that's what Taylor was and knew not to ask about what he was doing alone in the desert.

Sue was a hit right off. The guys unloaded the packs and found food for him. Everyone wanted to pet him.

Taylor was enjoying his beer while watching the guys enjoy Sue when a soldier approached him. "One of my guys said you were from Arkansas. I'm Jack Greer from Sumter. My dad is your age. His name is

Luke. I don't suppose you know him." Jack asked as he shook Taylor's hand.

"I know your dad. We're good friends. I grew up about five miles from Sumter. What a small world," Taylor said.

"You won't believe this, but the boss is also from Arkansas. He has procured a quantity of prime beef steaks that will melt in your mouth. Come with me, and I'll show you around. Don't worry about Sue. The guys will take care of him."

Luke informed Taylor they must stop at the boss' tent on their way to the chow hall.

Luke saluted the boss and introduced Taylor. "I understand you're from Arkansas. I'm from Crossett," the boss said as they shook hands.

"Yes sir, I live in northwest Arkansas now, but I was born and grew up in Sumter. While on leave about this time last year, I was sitting in a duck blind on Big Mossy Lake shooting Mallard ducks," Taylor said.

"I'll be damn, Big Mossy isn't ten miles from where I grew up and lived until I was eighteen. I miss duck hunting. We should plan a hunting trip when we return to the States.

It's nice to meet you, Taylor. Welcome to our little shindig. Sergeant, make sure this man gets a good steak and enjoys the festivities."

A plate was prepared for him in the kitchen, and he sat down with Jack and a group of soldiers.

"Jack, you weren't BS-ing me. This may be the best steak I've ever had. "The 75th never fed us like this," he joked.

That started the war stories. Some were on the edge of disbelief, but having been down several of those roads himself, Taylor knew they were real. After being with the guys for just a few hours, he felt he had never left the Army.

***

In the distance, the sound of a helicopter resonated across the valley. At the same time, on cue, the classic song from Toby Keith, "The Red, White and blue," comes blasting from a large set of speakers.

As the Blackhawk approached, two women on each side leaned out of the chopper's open doors. They were wearing military fatigues. A couple of them had bandoliers of ammo draped across their chests.

The guys had strict orders to not touch the girls but let them interact however they wanted. After landing, the four women lined up in front of the Blackhawk and seductively started removing all of their battle gear to the music and cheers from the men. After shedding everything down to their camouflaged pants, tee shirts, and combat boots, they fearlessly walked into the group of men. They hugged and kissed every one of the twenty guys.

After twenty minutes of mingling with the guys, the girls made their way to the makeshift band stage. Before starting their show, they lined up again in front of the helicopter, each holding a shot glass of whiskey. They raised their glasses to the guys for a salute, "strength and honor," they shouted before downing their shots in one slug.

The drummer started the rhythmic clicking of

her drumsticks. At the same time, the other band members got their guitars tuned and the sound levels adjusted.

The girls played every song shouted to them for over two hours. They were good, really good. From country to rock and roll, they sang and played their hearts out.

It was a helluva show.

The girls flew off into the last rays of sunlight, sitting in the open doorway with their boots swinging in the air while waving to the guys.

Suddenly, the chopper banked sharply, returned to the camp, and landed. With the engines still running and the rotor blades still turning, the girls jumped from the chopper and ran through the guys again, hugging everyone before they left for good.

This war story would be remembered for the rest of their lives.

The girls were gone, but the guys were still wired. "Hey, sarge, we have a few bottles of the hard stuff. What's your pleasure?" one of the guys asked.

"Scotch would be great," Taylor replied.

He was handed a plastic cup with a double shot of scotch and a cigar.

"Damn, you guys make me want to re-up," he said, laughing.

Not to let the party cool off, a soldier who was a good singer and a couple of other guys who could play the guitar took the stage and continued the entertainment.

After another couple of hours, it was getting late.

With enough war stories and scotch for the evening, Taylor excused himself to check on Sue and get some rest before he headed out early the next morning.

From his tent, he checked in with Kathryn to get an update on any new data.

While waiting for her response, he thought about his time with the guys. At first, he didn't think this get-together would be a good idea. The guys would probably not like a stranger in their tight circle. He chuckled at the thought that the guys seemed to genuinely like him, or was it Sue they liked, and he just happened to be along with him. Whatever the reason, he was glad he went. He made new friends. He mused that with most of them, he could be their father.

The guys joked about it but, at the same time, were serious. If he gets in a bind and needs help, just pick up the phone and call them. They gave him their radio call sign.

After leaving camp early the next morning and walking steadily all day, he was bone tired. He set up camp early to get a good night's rest. He removed the packs from Sue and fed and watered him. He set up camp and had an MRE dinner.

He received an update from Kathryn. There was no significant intel that would affect him.

It was a couple of hours before dark. He was leaning back against his sleeping bag draped over one of the packs Sue was carrying and relaxing as he watched a hawk circle overhead.

He was in the middle of a daydream when, out of

nowhere, he heard gunfire. He grabbed his weapon and binoculars and eased to the edge of the canyon wall where he could overlook the canyon floor below him.

Two men were using a pickup truck as a shield as they fired from behind it. A hundred yards away, there were several vehicles and a group of men returning their fire.

Suddenly bullets were ricocheting off the rocks beside him. Trying to outflank the guys behind the pickup, two guys from the opposing group ran head-on into Taylor's camp. Assuming Taylor was with the guys in the pickup, they attacked him. There was nothing he could do but protect himself. The two men were out in the open, firing and advancing on his position. With no other choice, he shot both men.

He positioned himself to see if more men were coming up to him., but after a time, the opposing group retreated and left the canyon.

An hour had passed with no gunfire. He watched as the other men got in their truck and drove away from the area, leaving his line of sight.

Another hour had passed when he heard a vehicle clawing and banging its way up the bolder-strewn and washed-out road leading to his position.

Taylor was prepared to shoot whoever it was if necessary. When the vehicle appeared, it was the pickup. He was hidden behind a large rock and had his weapon on his shoulder.

Both men exited their truck and started to walk toward Sue.

They were shocked to see Taylor and ran for cover behind their vehicle. Taylor fired a round over their heads and yelled, "Stop! Get on the ground." Not knowing if they spoke English, he gestured for them to get on their knees and not move.

With his weapon trained on them, and after they had complied with his demands, "English?" he asked.

"Yes," they both stammered at the same time.

"Who are you, and what was this fight about?" Taylor asked.

"We were checking on a complaint from a village elder that his sheep were being stolen. We caught the thieves in the act, which started the fight."

"Who's your boss?" Taylor asked.

"Abdul-Hadi," one responded.

Taylor couldn't believe this development. If these guys connect him with Abdul, it could compromise his plan. The thought crossed his mind that he should kill them, but he knew it was not in him to do that.

He had one man tie the other one's hands behind his back. Then, with his pistol in one hand, he tied the other guy's hands behind his back and then tied them together back-to-back.

After running several options through his head for over an hour, he devised a plan.

He showed the men a map and pointed to the primitive campsite where he had spent the night on his way to meet Abdul for the first time. After noting several landmarks on the map in the area of the camp, the men agreed they knew the place and could find their way there.

He told them he would let them go if they went directly to the camp and stayed there until someone came for them. He made it clear that they would be tracked by a satellite, and a drone would kill them if they did not go straight there.

He released the men, watched them drive down to the canyon floor, and head in the direction Taylor ordered them to take.

He contacted Kathryn, told her of the incident, and asked her to contact Abdul and have him pick the men up. A few hours later, she texted that she had contacted Abdul. He said he would take care of the men.

She also noted that Abdul was well and recovering from his wound.

CHAPTER XXXI

to kill a warlord

Early the next morning, he continued his trek. After two more days of steady walking, he arrived at the base of the hill overlooking the village.

He took a worn path winding up the side of the hill that ended at the top overlooking the village. Taylor unloaded Sue and carried his gear to a place he had selected down the hill toward the village. It was out of sight of anyone coming up the path behind him.

He told Sue how much he appreciated his help and companionship. He scratched his ears and neck, then patted him on his rump, signaling him to go back down the hill and to the cave.

It took several hours to position his gear. It could be days or never to get a shot at Rahid. He placed his clothing and sleeping bag under an overhanging ledge of rock. He attached a camouflaged tarp to the ledge face with rock climbing cams and secured the bottom with a couple of large stones to give him more covered space.

He carefully checked the sniper rifle and scope,

ensuring it was working properly and ready to fire. He opened the scope lens protectors and gently cleaned the lens of any debris. He inserted a full magazine of bullets into the firearms mag well. He worked the bolt to load a bullet into the chamber and moved the firing selector to the safe position. He folded out the bipod attached to the forearm and adjusted it to a comfortable firing position.

He spread a poncho on the ground to make it comfortable to aim and fire the weapon, knowing there was a probability he could be there for days.

Lying down with the rifle against his shoulder in firing position and looking through the scope, he was satisfied everything was in order and ready to go. He opened an MRE and a bottle of water.

After eating, he opened his laptop and contacted Kathryn. He had reached his destination and was ready to proceed with their plan. She updated him on the latest data on Rahid, which was limited to intercepted electronic chatter.

They didn't know where he was, but a drone had been dedicated to search for him. And they discussed the maximum amount of time he should wait for Rahid before extracting him. The human body could stay in a high-stress state for just so long.

He had received the satellite topography map of the village. He matched what he could see with his night-vision binoculars to the map. Scanning the village, he could see dogs moving around inside the compound, two motorcycles parked against the compound wall, and a stone water well. He saw where he had been confined. Over the next hour, he familiarized himself with the compound.

He would watch through the day to see if anyone made their way to the tower. Even with binoculars, he was too far away to identify Rahib. He needed to find a location as close as possible to the village where he could place a video camera that he could monitor from his laptop to identify Rahid.

He watched the daily routine of the village. Young boys played soccer while the girls played a board game in the shadow of a tree. For additional shade, there was a white canvas tarp tied to the tree's limbs and the post supporting the porch of the building.

The center of activity was the stone water well in the middle of the compound. Someone was constantly lowering the wooden bucket attached to a rope and pulley system into the well to retrieve the water. They washed clothes, filled a metal container for the animals, and irrigated a vegetable garden. Individuals would drink from the bucket with a long-handled dipper.

He tried to stay alert but catnapped throughout the day. It was after midnight when he headed for the village. It was a dark night with no moon, so it would be difficult for anyone to see him.

With his night-vision goggles on, he descended the hill to a line of scraggly trees. They were growing outside the far wall of the compound but right up against it. He chose a tree to give the camera a good field of view and strapped it onto a limb.

He was slowly climbing down from the tree when

a door opened, and a woman with a child walked to the outdoor toilet. He froze as the two village dogs woke and followed the woman. He was in an awkward position, which made one leg go numb. But he knew to not move a muscle for fear of the dogs spotting him. Finally, the woman returned to her room, and the dogs wandered to the other side of the courtyard and lay down.

Taylor waited another few minutes before climbing down from the tree and returning to his place on the hill. He was relieved the village dogs hadn't smelled him and started barking.

He retired to his sleeping bag for a few hours before daylight. He woke to rain pattering on his makeshift lean-to. He was glad he made the extra effort to build it. He was dry and had enough room to move around, making it much more comfortable.

It was light enough to see the village. He checked his laptop to see if the wireless camera was working. He could see the dogs walking around inside the compound, confirming it was working properly.

He made a hot cup of coffee with a container of gel fuel that didn't give off any smoke. He had jury-rigged his binoculars to his camera tripod with parachute cord, so he didn't have to constantly hold the binoculars while monitoring the compound. He also had made a comfortable backrest with his duffel bag.

He rechecked his weapon. His range finder indicated the water well was 732 feet from him. He removed the scope dust covers and adjusted the elevation knob according to the ballistics data of the bullets he would be using.

Now it was a waiting game. A drone had been dedicated to the area. It would send an alarm if a vehicle approached the village. He must stay alert. The window of opportunity may exist for only a few minutes.

It was day five and becoming increasingly difficult to stay alert. He was sound asleep when the drone alerted him to a vehicle approaching the village. Fortunately, it wasn't Rahid, or he may not have been able to make the shot.

He looked forward to the night so he could leave his shelter, walk the path for exercise, and clear his mind.

One night, he heard something below him stirring in the dark as he walked. Alarmed, he took his pistol from his shoulder holster and lowered his night vision goggles to his eyes. It was two wild mountain goats foraging through the rocks for food.

Back at camp, he was settling in for the night when Kathryn sent him a message. "There is intel indicating Rahid may be in the area. The command center has deployed a helicopter five miles from your location. The helicopter will be able to follow events in real-time. If they spot a vehicle heading to the village, they will get airborne and be ready to pick you up."

It had been determined that if Taylor took a shot, he would descend to a small flat area in the pathway down from the top of the hill. The helicopter could pick him up there without being exposed to fire from the village.

He spent the next two hours packing up. He moved everything to the helicopter pickup point except for the sniper rifle and laptop. He was to leave nothing that would indicate his presence.

He had slept maybe three hours before daylight came, but he was alert, feeling this could be the day. If Rahid didn't show up today, he would have to seriously consider giving up.

He double-checked every detail of his rifle and settled in with high expectations. He looked into the village and the surrounding landscape with binoculars for any unusual activity.

Hours passed. Disheartened, he was drinking a bottle of water, wishing it was scotch, when his laptop alarm flashed, indicating the drone had spotted a vehicle moving toward the village.

Taylor moved into a firing position, switched on the laptop to monitor the video camera he had placed in the tree, and waited for the vehicle to enter the village. Upon entering the compound, the rifle scope's crosshairs followed the vehicle until it stopped. Taylor eased his finger to the trigger. But then the vehicle moved below his line of sight behind the wall.

On the other side of the compound, the camera could see the area of the blind spot. Taylor watched the camera feed as people left the vehicle and entered the building.

Their backs were to him, so he couldn't identify them. Time was running out. It will be dark in a couple of hours. Finally, the door opened, and the camera displayed Rahid talking to a group of people. He was wearing a black dishdasha. But Rahid unwittingly never presented himself for a shot.

Taylor watched the camera view as Rahid got into his vehicle. After the vehicle exited the compound about fifty yards, Taylor fired multiple rounds of armor-piercing bullets into the vehicle, trying to hit the engine, tires, or the people in it.

He couldn't tell if he had hit anything, but the vehicle stopped. Nothing happened for a few seconds, then it exploded in a ball of fire.

Taylor knew by the explosion that the vehicle had been hit by a Rocket Propelled Grenade.

He grabbed his binoculars and scanned the area around the vehicle. Villagers were coming out to see what had happened.

Several vehicles came into view as he watched the villagers through his binoculars. Two were pickup trucks full of soldiers with AK-47 rifles and RPGs. The third vehicle was a white Mercedes.

It stopped close to the burning vehicle, and Abdul exited the passenger side door on crutches.

Taylor watched closely as Abdul talked to the villagers.

After a while, he returned to his SUV, but before he got in, he turned toward the hill Taylor was on and gave him the finger.

Taylor made his way down the backside of the hill, where a helicopter was waiting for him. He retrieved his stowed gear and handed it to a crew member. He pulled himself in, and the chopper lifted off.

CHAPTER XXXII

celebrate successful operation

Regardless of Abdul's efforts to keep the location of his cave complex a secret, Taylor had traveled the area enough that he could return to the cave if he wanted. But Abdul would be angry with him if he revealed the location of his cave to the CIA. So, he directed the chopper pilot to where Abdul's bodyguards picked him up the first time he came from Erbil. After he unloaded his gear, the chopper left.

He hid his gear in some rocks except for his rifle, handgun, a small backpack to carry his laptop, and a couple bottles of water. He would have Abdul return for the rest of his gear sometime later.

With the moon lighting the way, he started walking toward the cave. The road was barely visible, with little more than tire tracks in the desert sand.

It was midnight when headlights appeared in the distance coming toward him. He quickly moved off the road a few yards and lay down in a small depression that would make it difficult to see him.

Every stripe of outlaw, from drug dealers to

heartless, cold-blooded bandits, roamed the region. This was the time of night when they were out.

A white Mercedes passed by him. Abdul had read his mind. He walked to the middle of the road and directed his flashlight toward the vehicle flashing it off and on. The vehicle stopped. It didn't move for a minute before it turned around and came toward him. He checked his rifle and moved the selector from safe to fire.

The SUV window came down, "Lawton, are you suicidal? There is no other place on this planet that an American would be more likely to get his head cut off than right here."

"I'm looking for a bar with thirty-year-old scotch and women of the same age," Taylor said.

"I was sure this is where you would be, but I'm surprised to find you walking in the night. You are fearless or insane," Abdul said.

"I left most of my gear at the campsite. I figured I could have your guys take me back to pick it up."

"It is late. Get in. I will send someone for your stuff tomorrow. But, right now, I need something to drink and rest my aching hip that you did such a lousy job of sewing up. That's why the finger, you did see it, didn't you," Abdul said.

"Yeah, I never thought I would be patching a hole in your sorry ass."

Relaxing in Abdul's tent outside the cave, they recalled the events leading to killing Rahid.

"The timing of your stopping Rahid's vehicle was incredible. Hitting a moving target with an RPG is difficult. As far away as we were from him, it would have been tough. After trying several times to hit him, I figured we would have to chase him down, and many people would be killed. When I heard the gunshots echo across the valley and Rahid's vehicle stopped, I knew it was the infidel," Abdul smirked.

"It does seem that the stars lined up for us. I couldn't get a shot at him in the compound and was just trying to stop his vehicle. I figured he would be too smart to get out of his vehicle and give me a clear shot but wait for the villagers to come after me. "Then, out of nowhere, you smoked his ass," Taylor said.

Taylor stayed a few more days writing and discussing Abdul's future. It was improbable that the person he came to Iraq to kill was now someone he had grown to respect and consider a friend. His gear was loaded. He was ready to leave.

Abdul handed him his personal pistol. "Set this beside your keyboard as you write your story. It will help you remember our adventure more intensely.

"At one time, I seriously considered shooting you with this," Abdul said.

"After you read my story, you may want it back," Taylor joked.

They embraced.

The Mercedes faded into the desert.

CHAPTER XXXIII

return to the US

In Cyprus, Taylor met with a CIA operative for a lengthy debriefing. Then, he met Ed at the marina. They had been invited to a dinner party at the dock pavilion. They had a pleasant evening talking with folks from all over the world.

They returned to Ed's boat and continued discussing their adventure.

It was time to start thinking about returning to the US. Ed offered that he would understand if Taylor preferred to fly back to the States instead of sailing. He had made the trip solo many times before.

"Heck no, unless you want to have that time to yourself, I'm looking forward to the trip," Taylor said.

Kathryn would be back in Cyprus in a couple of days. He looked forward to spending as much time with her as possible before he and Ed returned to the States. They met at the sidewalk café across from the US Embassy where they first met.

Taylor stood and welcomed her with an affectionate kiss.

"Hey, beautiful."

"Mr. Lawton, how are you?"

"My nickname is Infidel. That's what Abdul calls me," Taylor said.

"Speaking of Abdul, I just left an intel briefing concerning him. You will be pleased to know he is well and has consolidated his control over Rahid's province."

They talked, recalling their adventure together, and made plans to spend the evening together.

"Ed and I will head back to the States pretty soon. I was hoping you would have some time to spend together before we leave."

***

After an hour and a half flight, Kathryn landed the airplane on the island of Crete. From the airport, they took a taxi to a Villa on the north shore. After settling in, they had cocktails on the veranda overlooking the ocean.

"Macallan, you certainly are well connected. I've never been in a place like this except when I went into one of Saddam Hussein's palaces after we kicked his ass," he remarked as they touched glasses.

"Did you bring my favorite massage lotion?" she asked seductively.

They decided to walk to a marina down the beach a short distance away.

"We must keep our "marina ploy" a secret," Kathryn said as they made their way down the dock walkway.

Predictably, after visiting with several people

lounging on the aft deck of their boat, they were invited to come aboard for a cocktail. A couple of boats later, they were invited to the customary dock party set for the evening.

After dinner and a sunset cruise, they walked on the beach back to the Villa. They sat on a couple of beach chairs and drank wine Taylor had chilled for the occasion.

"I'm still thinking about that getaway cruise. This looks like the perfect sunset to sail into," she sighed.

Their time together was short because of Kathryn's demanding schedule, and they returned to Cyprus after a few days. They spent a few more evenings together back in Cyprus. But the day came, and it was time for Taylor and Ed to leave for the US.

Taylor was standing on the aft deck of Ed's sailboat, looking intently at Kathryn as the boat slowly pulled away from the dock. She was leaning against a piling that supported the dock, holding a glass of wine by her side.

"When will I see you again?" he asked.

"They say Fólkvangr is beautiful in the fall," she said as she watched Taylor until the sailboat disappeared into the Mediterranean Sea.

CHAPTER XXXIV

back home

Taylor parked his truck, walked across the street, took the stairs down to Lojos restaurant and entered.

"Taylor Lawton, it is good to see you my friend. You must be a true blue-water sailor by now?" Tom, the bar owner, said.

"Hey Tommy, it's good to see you. Yeah, my buddy Ed and I have seen a lot of saltwater over the last year. It was quite an experience," Taylor responded.

He didn't call any of his friends to meet him. He just wanted to sit quietly at the end of the bar, recall his adventure, and contemplate the future. It was early afternoon. Not many people were in the bar.

Back home, he sat down at his PC and continued chronicling his adventure. He had gotten into writing, spending hours typing and recalling events of his adventure.

***

Back home for five months he enjoyed seeing family and friends. He talked with the local newspaper about publishing his article. They were somewhat interested after reading a rough draft.

It was still thirty minutes before daylight, but he could see well enough to maneuver his fishing boat through the stumps and trees with the trolling motor. He cast a lure as close to the bank as possible without getting it hung up in the brush lining the bank. He never tired of watching the top-water lure sit motionless on the surface of the still water until the slightest twitch of the rod triggered a black bass to attack the lure in an explosion of water.

The sun had been up for a couple of hours. He sat his fishing rod down and opened his laptop. It was early for a beer, but as Jimmy Buffett would say …

With his self-imposed rule of indulging only when hunting or fishing, he placed a pinch of smokeless tobacco in his cheek after finishing his beer and started typing an email.

Kathryn,

I'm on my favorite lake trying to catch enough fish to feed a few friends coming to my dock for a cookout this evening. You know, fishing and cooking are my favorite interests. Oh, and there is this woman. Everything is good except for one minor problem. I constantly daydream of being back in the hunt. I was looking forward to returning to the retired syndrome, but now that I have had time to reflect on what we have accomplished, I'm having second thoughts regarding my future.

We have developed a relationship with an influential faction in Iraq. I think it would be a lost opportunity not to continue our work. Also, I will confess that I have become addicted to the adrenaline rush of the hunt.

I plan to contact Abdul, return to Iraq, and continue developing the alliance we were working on when I left. And unless he's had a major change of heart, I am the only "infidel" he will work with anyway. And, of course, your organization agreeing to my plan will be essential.

If this happens, we will have to put off that Australia trip, but not being above a bribe, I have this special lotion.

Soon enough,
Taylor

He contacted Ed to see if he was interested in returning to Iraq. "I've been expecting your call. I haven't unpacked my bags," he joked.

He did his best to explain to his son and daughter why he was returning to Cyprus without disclosing classified data. He told them he had run into some old Army buddies working for a Private Military Contractor and had convinced Ed and him to join their group for the adventure and great pay. Everything was true, except they would form their own two-man PMC company.

Everyone at Lojos was surprised at the news of Taylor planning another sailing trip.

"Man, you should be thinking about fishing, watching football, and a good recliner," Tom joked.

"The sailing trip with Ed did something to my soul. I felt like I was thirty years old again after experiencing the exhilaration of the sailboat heeling over so far that I could run my fingers in the ocean. The spray from the waves drenching me from head to toe, and the briny taste of seawater evoking that primal bond with the ocean was something to experience deep down in my soul.

"I'm a pirate looking at Fifty, and I don't want to be late or a victim of fate. Where in the hell is Buffett? I want to buy him a Margarita," Taylor said.

"It has motivated me to take, in all probability, that last shot at the adventure of a lifetime.

"My father often quoted Chaucer's "Time and tide wait for no man."

The sailing trip back to Cyprus wasn't as easy as the first trip. Halfway between Bermuda and the Azores, they found themselves in a storm that lasted two days.

The boat had three bilge pumps, two electric and one manual. The two electric pumps failed, so they were reduced to bailing water with the manual pump. Ed drove tapered wooden pegs into the useless hull drain holes to keep more water from entering the boat.

Below deck, Taylor operated the manual pump. Ed tethered himself to the helm to prevent being washed overboard as he steered the boat into the wind to keep it from capsizing. They continued the process for hours. And to make matters worse, Taylor got seasick from being below deck with the boat pitching wildly in the roiling waves.

Then it was over, with patches of blue sky and a not-so-angry sea.

"I think Poseidon wanted to see what you're made of. You passed the test, which consists of simply surviving the storm. We should celebrate your joining an exclusive club of sailors with a shot of whiskey," Ed said.

"I have confronted fear many times in my life, but the pure terror I experienced with this storm is at the top of the list. This Poseidon fellow is not someone to mess with," Taylor joked.

They returned to the same marina.

CHAPTER XXXV

return to Iraq

Taylor was at the sidewalk café across from the US Embassy, where he first met Kathryn. "A dirty vodka martini on the rocks in a cocktail glass and a glass of your best Syrah, please." He said to the waiter.

He could see her coming from a distance. He was excited to see her but felt awkward at the same time. But he should have known not to be concerned. "Déjà vu, my darling," she said in her best French brogue.

"So, you are happy to see me?" Taylor quipped.

"Not so much you as the wine," she said as she kissed him.

"I know your taste," he replied.

They enjoyed their drinks and rejoined conversation. "It is a beautiful day, let's walk," she suggested.

They leisurely strolled through the streets to the marina where Ed's boat was docked. There were people whom they had met on their first trip and invited them to join the perpetual dock party. After dining they took the requisite tour of a new sailboat the owners were proud of and wanted everyone to see.

Into the fading afternoon pleasantries, they took their leave. They hailed a taxi and went to Kathryn's suite. "What were you drinking at the café?" she asked.

"Dirty vodka martini on the rocks," he replied.

"Another or scotch?" she asked as she headed to the kitchen.

"I will stick with Vodka," he said.

On the Veranda, he had pulled two lounge chairs together while she was making the drinks. He was leaning back in one of the chairs when she brought the beverages. "Your cocktail tasted so good I made one for myself," she said as she handed him his drink.

After taking a sip, "This is the best vodka. It must be expensive. But wait, it's the lipstick. What vintage is this?" he laughed.

"How about some LaMontagne and savor the rest of the evening doing nothing but you giving me a massage that I have sorely missed. We have tomorrow to talk shop," she said, laying back in her lounge chair.

The next morning, they began discussing several operations that would be suitable for Taylor to take on. Kathryn gave him a prioritized list of operations the CIA believed would be best handled by a Private Military Contractor.

She suggested Taylor meet with Abdul to see if any of their priorities aligned with what he was working on or would have an interest in.

***

After the fight with Rahid, Abdul had decided the

cave was too important as a weapon and ammunition depot to live there and possibly expose it to the enemy. He had moved to an abandoned village a few miles up the river from the cave. The village was also more centrally located now that his area of control had expanded due to taking over Rahid's province.

Abdul seemed genuinely pleased to see him. "As you see, I have moved my headquarters. It was necessary because of security issues."

He showed Taylor around his new headquarters. "Infidel, you are burning through your cat of nine lives coming back here. I was quite sure you were mad, and this confirms it. I fight for my country, but you are just an evil mercenary," he jeered.

"I'm a mercenary only if you compensate me for working for you. So how many dinars are you planning to pay me? And speaking of compensation, I have a bill for sewing up that hole in your ass," Taylor quipped.

"Come walk with me. We will talk about our future collaboration. The factions wanting to control Iraq are like chameleons. They change allegiances every day, so I have a new adversary every day. I have been thinking about our working together since you said you were returning to Iraq," Abdul said.

CHAPTER XXXVI

new terrorist target

They walked to the riverbank and reminisced about the past before Abdul commented on their future alliance. "The number one power broker today is an Iranian named Hamud Ben Maldih. He is responsible for more coalition deaths than anyone else, and I know he is on the US's shit list. We should work together to capture him. The information he could provide would be invaluable to the coalition," Abdul said.

"Do you know where he is now?" Taylor asked.

"I don't have the technology to track him like you do. But a week ago, he was in Baghdad, which is the latest information I have."

"I will request an update on him from my people, and we will start putting a plan together," Taylor replied.

He advised Kathryn of Abdul's proposal regarding Hamud Ben Maldih.

A few days later, Kathryn contacted Taylor. "Intel has Hamud going to Beirut on the twenty-first of next month for a meeting with a consortium of arms dealers. The event will be held at the mansion of Beirut's top crime boss, Victor Konjanko. He enjoys throwing large parties and inviting the rich and powerful. So that gives us six weeks to plan his capture," Kathryn said.

Taylor informed Abdul of the information. "I have contacts in Beirut. I will work on getting people on the wait staff to inform us about what is going on," Abdul said.

"That would be very useful," Taylor replied.

After returning to Cyprus, Taylor met Kathryn at the embassy and started working on a plan to capture Hamud.

"The CIA has had Hamud under surveillance for years. We have an extensive dossier on him. There have been circumstances in the past where we worked with him fighting a mutual enemy.

"But the last few years have seen him turn increasingly to the terrorist mindset. We know a great deal about his conventions which are typical of men of his narcissistic character. He enjoys flaunting his power and influence at events such as this one. And people who oppose him often disappear. He enjoys using his position at events like this one to seduce the female wait staff by offering large sums of money for them to have sex with him. They are flattered by a man of his position, and the money he offers makes it difficult to decline.

"He will slip away from the party just long enough for a brief tryst. He has been to parties at Konjanko's mansion before and always stays in a separate chalet a few yards from the main house. This may be the penchant to exploit," Kathryn said.

"So, what are your thoughts regarding this affinity?" Taylor asked.

"Obviously, a female operative posing as a member of the wait staff that could draw his attention and entice him to offer his money for sex ploy sounds like a viable plan. If we could lure him away from the party and to his chalet, it would allow us to discretely take him down," Kathryn replied.

"And where are you going to find this femme fatale," Taylor joked.

"I want to do it," Kathryn said.

"I knew you would say that, and my initial reaction to that idea is hell no. But the fact is, you are the most qualified person to take this on, and you would tell me to stuff it anyway. How may Ed and I help?"

"You can drive the get-a-way vehicle and boat. Familiarize yourself with the city streets and the route to the boat that will take us to Cyprus. Ed will follow behind us to add a backup in case we run into trouble," Kathryn suggested.

"Hamud likes to seduce the woman he chooses by flirting with her to get her reaction. If he likes her, he will have one of his people approach her and forward his request. I will have one shot at enticing him to take me to his chalet, where two special forces operators will be waiting to capture him.

"Once we have Hamud, the clock will start ticking. When his people realize he has not returned from his tryst, they will start looking for him. When they figure out he has been abducted, his people will immediately demand the authorities start a search for him," Kathryn said.

The next evening, Taylor and Kathryn took a taxi to the boat they would use to take them to Cyprus. The boat was in a narrow canal with other boats docked on both sides. It was tied up alongside a wooden dock a few yards from a private villa.

Taylor had driven boats similar to this one but wanted to familiarize himself with the controls of this particular craft. He also wanted to navigate the canal and bay in the dark to familiarize himself with the route to the open ocean. He spent an hour checking out everything he could think of regarding the operation of the boat.

After waiting for dark, he started the engines, disconnected the shore power, released the dock lines, and used the bow thrusters to move away from the dock.

Following the navigation buoys, he progressed through the bay into the ocean.

"Well, what do you think? The canal is pretty narrow. Are you confident you can navigate it at night under stress?" Kathryn asked.

"I will have a few beers while waiting in the get-a-way vehicle at Konjanko's house. Then, I will be ready to roll when we get to the boat," he joked. "But seriously, I'm good after this practice run."

The ocean was placid, so Taylor took the boat out of gear and let it drift with the current. "I worry that something may go wrong with your dealing with this Hamud bastard," he argued.

"I appreciate your concern, but I hand-picked the guys for this operation. And let me assure you, they are truly badass. If anything goes wrong, they will kill Hamud."

"I will try to quit worrying about it," Taylor said.

"Let's not waste anymore of this beautiful evening. Search your phone for a restaurant on the water," he suggested.

Kathryn found a restaurant that had a dock with slips for customers. They had a pleasant dinner, then walked on the beach enjoying the cool air of an approaching storm. Miles out to sea, shards of lightning shattered the ominous clouds. They bought a bottle of wine and returned to the boat.

They motored from the pier and again drifted down the coast toward the marina. After a glass of wine, Kathryn decided she wanted to swim. She stripped off her clothes and dove into the water before Taylor could say anything.

"Don't be a prig, Lawton. Jump in," she said, chiding him.

"You know sharks feed at night, plus I have a better view of your pretty ass from the boat. I will watch for sharks and pirates," he said, laughing.

After swimming for a few minutes, she climbed the swim ladder and went to the boat's bow. There was a large lounge cushion for sunbathing, and she lay on her stomach, "Backrub, please."

Taylor brought her a glass of wine and massaged

her from head to toe.

"Okay, you've convinced me. Fire this thing up and head for Australia and a Lemon Myrtle cocktail," she sighed.

CHAPTER XXXVII

terrorist abducted

Konjanko used an event contractor to supply and coordinate everything from food preparation to the red carpet.

Kathryn applied to work as a waiter at the event. She and twenty other men and women were selected for the occasion. She dressed as sexy as possible in her waitress uniform without being too obvious.

Konjanko's house was a remarkable place. Built in the colonial era, the compound comprised a city block. Workers were rushing around completing the final details: red carpet, stocking the bar, fresh flowers, cleaning and edging the driveway, etc.

Limousines were in line all the way to the gated entrance. It looked like the opening of a Broadway play. The ballroom was packed. The band played as heavy hitters vied for positions of influence and power.

An hour into the party, Kathryn approached Hamud with a tray of champagne. He was talking to a couple of men and a woman. She offered the flutes of champagne to the group and smiled at Hamud as he took a glass.

Moving to another group of people, she tried to determine with her peripheral vision if he was checking her out.

Thirty minutes later, Kathryn was loading another tray with Champagne when her supervisor approached her. "Terry, right?"

"Yes," Kathryn said, answering to her phony name.

"I would like to talk to you for a minute."

"Sure, what's up?"

"Do you know Mr. Hamud?"

"I have no idea who any of these people are."

"He is very wealthy," she said.

"A handsome, wealthy guy, I may be in love already. Why are you telling me this?" Kathryn asked.

"I met Hamud at a party like this a few years ago. He asked about one of the waitresses that he was interested in. He said he would pay me a hundred dollars if I had the girl bring a bottle of champagne to him at the swimming pool, where he would offer to pay her to have sex with him. He promised me he would never hurt a woman that turned him down. Two girls, at separate times, have told me he gave them five hundred dollars."

"Five hundred bucks, that's two months' income for me," Kathryn said.

"He is interested in you. Would you have sex with him for five hundred dollars?"

Not wanting to sound too eager, Kathryn asked more questions about Hamud before asking for a few minutes to consider the offer. She made another round of the room with a tray of drinks before agreeing to the proposition. "I could certainly use 500 bucks. I will do it."

Kathryn took a break on the terrace to review the operation details and mentally prepare for the task before meeting Hamud. Walking to the pool with a bottle of champagne and two glasses, she saw Hamud waiting for her. "Hi Terry, thank you for bringing me a bottle of champagne. Please, have a glass with me," he said.

He removed the cork and filled his and her glass. "Thank you," she replied.

"You are a pretty girl."

She smiled.

"Do you have any questions about what Paula discussed with you?" "No," she replied.

"My quarters are just down the path. Let's enjoy each other for a while," he said, taking her hand.

Kathryn's heart rate was going up. What if her guys aren't there for some reason? Would Hamud let her return to the main house if she told him she had changed her mind? Could she physically resist if necessary?

Hamud unlocked and opened the door to the chalet. Out of nowhere, one of the operators slammed him in the back so hard he was knocked off his feet. Immediately, the second operator tasered him and stabbed a syringe of anesthesia into his abdomen. In less than thirty seconds, Hamud was unconscious.

Kathryn changed out of her waitress uniform.

"Lock the front door, Kat. We're going out the back," an operator said. The two operators grabbed Hamud's arms and dragged him toward the back door. "Open the door for us, then lock it behind you."

Everyone exited the house, and Kathryn locked the door.

Hamud was loaded into a golf cart, and they drove to the back of the property, where a gate was in the stone fence. Kathryn opened the gate to check if Taylor was waiting in the get-a-way vehicle. He was in a parking lot on the other side of the street to avoid suspicion. She signaled Taylor with a flashlight that they were ready to go.

As soon as the vehicle pulled up, they loaded Hamud into the back of the SUV and started driving down the street. They headed into the city with Ed close behind, ready for any conflict.

It was a forty-five-minute drive through the city to reach the boat. Taylor was careful to drive as normally as possible to not draw attention.

They drove close to the dock and boarded the boat carrying the still-unconscious Hamud.

Taylor started the engines and cast off the lines. He maneuvered the boat through the canal and out to sea. The boat had been modified so Hamud, still sedated, could be hidden behind a false bulkhead. They knew the Beirut police and Lebanese Coast Guard had been alerted by now and were watching the airport and marinas.

If they made a run for Cyprus, they would likely be caught before they could get to international waters, where a US warship and aircraft could protect them. As soon as they reached a location known for good fishing, they rigged two rods and started fishing.

Thirty minutes later, they saw a boat approaching. It was the Lebanese Coast Guard.

The op guys were prepared for a fight if it came to that. They had weapons hidden but close at hand.

Coast guard personnel lowered a dinghy into the water, and four officials motored up close to their boat. A coast guard sailor threw a line to one of the operators and tied the two crafts together so the coast guard guys could board their boat.

An operator wearing Bermuda shorts and holding a beer waved to them.

"Request to board your vessel," an officer said.

"Is there a problem?" an operator asked.

With no comment, three Coast Guard officials came aboard. "Give me your registration papers. We will search your boat.

An operator handed over the registration papers.

An official entered the salon and looked around. Then, he began searching the three bedrooms. After searching two bedrooms, he opened the third cabin door and saw Kathryn asleep on the bed nude. Looking at her, he hesitated as long as possible before closing the door. The other Coast Guard officials had searched the engine room, crew quarters, and the live well where a couple of fish had been placed for just this situation.

"Have you seen other boats in this area in the last few hours?" an officer asked.

"I've seen the navigation lights on a couple of boats, but they were so far away I couldn't tell you anything about them," an operator said.

As the Coast Guard patrol boat pulled away, everyone breathed a sigh of relief.

"That was quick thinking, Kat, to distract that Coast Guard official. I want to be distracted when you decide to get naked again," one of the operators said, laughing.

"Okay, Taylor, haul ass to Cyprus," one of the operators said.

Taylor pushed the throttles full forward. The boat jumped up on plane and was quickly moving at forty knots.

They rendezvoused off the coast of Cyprus in international waters with an American warship. The ship sent a dinghy to pick up Hamud. He was awake but bewildered by what was happening. He was handcuffed and blindfolded, so he couldn't escape or recognize anyone. From there, he would be flown to Guantanamo Bay prison camp.

After transferring Hamud to the ship Taylor continued piloting the boat to Cyprus. They tied up to the dock, and Taylor turned the engines off.

There was a truck waiting to pick up the operators. Kathryn hugged and kissed both of them. "You guys did an amazing job. Hamud never knew what hit him."

The operators were shouldering their gear to leave, "Kat, don't forget to call us for your next nude scene, and Taylor, I'll kick your ass just for the hell of it the next time I see you," one of the operators said with a grin. Taylor waved, "Great job, guys."

With the two of them left on the boat, "Kat, huh?" Taylor asked.

"Yeah, one day someone used it, and it stuck. From then on, that was my name among friends and co-workers."

"Well, Kat Macallan, you did one helluva job on this operation.

CHAPTER XXXVIII

kidnapped

It had been three months since the successful Hamud operation. Taylor had rented a small apartment overlooking the marina. He was walking for the exercise and fresh air when he received a text from Ed inviting Kathryn and him to go sailing and have happy hour at the dock pavilion.

He texted Kathryn about the invitation, "Sounds good. What time?" she asked.

"Six?"

"That will work. I'm in a meeting with Matt at my hotel at the moment. You remember Matt, he was instrumental in persuading the CIA to help you with your venture. When the meeting with him is over, I must go to the embassy to pick up some documents before I go to Tel Aviv tomorrow. After that, I should have time to return to the hotel and dress for the evening," she replied.

Taylor texted Ed to accept his invitation. Kathryn and Matt finished their meeting, and she left for the embassy. Matt had a conference call after their meeting and stayed in the suite.

Taylor was looking forward to a day of solitude. Time to work on his manuscript had been limited with all the activity. Still, he was looking forward to the evening.

Kathryn returned to the hotel, assuming Matt had left. She put the key card into the door lock and entered the small foyer. She entered the adjacent room to find Matt on the floor with his head in a pool of blood. She knew by the color of the blood he had been dead for some time.

She called Taylor, "There's a problem. I must talk with you immediately. Can I come to your apartment at seven?" she asked.

Her voice told him something was terribly wrong.

"Sure, I'm in my apartment now."

Kathryn contacted the CIA. They removed the body and cleaned the suite of everything associated with Matt. The hotel and local police would never know of the incident.

She arrived at Taylor's apartment. He poured glasses of scotch, "Matt is dead," she said.

"The CIA has been concerned about Matt's safety for some time because there is intelligence that he was a target of Al-Radea. After the abduction of Hamud, Konjanko was furious to learn that the CIA was behind the kidnapping of Hamud from his private property. So, he hired a Russian mercenary to abduct Matt to negotiate a trade for Hamud.

"The Russian followed Matt to my hotel. He waited until I left, then tried to subdue Matt, but in the ensuing fight, the Russian killed him.

"I am going to kill Victor Konjanko," Kathryn said in a matter-of-fact tone.

Kathryn spent the next day being debriefed about Matt's death before she took a commercial flight to the States to attend his funeral.

When she returns to Cyprus, she was to meet with Taylor at his apartment to discuss plans to kill Konjanko.

***

Kathryn had not arrived or called an hour after their planned meeting time. Taylor called to check on her, but his call went to voicemail. He texted her, but there was no response. After two more hours and no word from Kathryn, he had a bad feeling. He checked with the airline to see if her flight had been canceled or was running late. The airline representative told him the airplane experienced mechanical problems and had to make an emergency landing at an alternate airport. The repairs had been made, and the aircraft should arrive in approximately two hours.

Relieved, he poured a drink and walked out onto his apartment deck. He tried to relax from worrying about Kathryn.

It was 2:00 am when the doorbell rang. Dazed from falling asleep on his couch, Taylor opened the door. A woman introduced herself as a representative of the US Embassy. Taylor knew without asking she was CIA and was there about Kathryn. He motioned for her to come in.

"Kathryn's airplane made an emergency landing at

an airport in ISIS-held territory due to mechanical problems. She was the only Caucasian on the flight and was abducted by ISIS intelligence.

"Kathryn had an undercover personal and business life created by the CIA. We hope her captors believe her story and see the value in her, otherwise, they will kill her. We should hear from her captors at any time if this turns into a hostage situation," the operator said.

"This is crazy. Do you have any information regarding Kathryn's location?" Taylor asked.

"We're using every available resource to rescue her," the agent responded.

"I will work with my sources also," Taylor said. He was already planning to contact Abdul for his help. If anyone could expedite the search for Kathryn, it would be Abdul.

"We anticipate contact with her captors at any time, but in the meantime, we should put every effort into finding her regardless of the situation. We will provide you with all the intel we develop and any equipment you request," she said.

Taylor and the agent discussed the situation at length before she left. "I have given you everything we know at this time," she said with tears in her eyes. "Kathryn is my friend. We must find her and bring her home."

Taylor was flown by helicopter to the old campsite he and Abdul had used several times. They had agreed that was where they would meet under such circumstances.

The helicopter took Taylor to the campsite and left.

He would go with Abdul to his camp.

Abdul arrived a few minutes later, and Taylor informed him of Kathryn's abduction. "We must find her as soon as possible and be ready to take action in case negotiations for her release fail," Taylor said.

Abdul could see the anxiety on Taylor's face, "I will start working on this immediately," he said.

CHAPTER XXXIX

escape

The ISIS interrogators concluded through their intelligence sources that Kathryn's undercover guise was legitimate and were convinced that she worked for a manufacturing company in Scotland.

They planned to trade her for a high-level ISIS leader in an Iraqi prison.

Kathryn's mind was coming out of the fog induced by the injection of drugs that had knocked her out. Lying on the floor, she opened her eyes and slowly returned to reality. She tried to recall what had happened. She sat up against the wall and started looking over her body. There were dark bruises on her shoulders and deep scratches on both forearms. Her wrists and ankles were red and bruised from being tied together.

Peering out of a window with steel bars in the mud brick wall of a small room, Kathryn could see another building. Because of the typical mud brick construction, she assumed she was still in Iraq. The wooden door to the room had the only other opening.

She strained from every angle to see what was on the other side of the door. She saw a covered portico extending the length of the building and a stone and mud wall with a large double gate at one end. She saw a guard tower in one corner of the compound. It was occupied by a single soldier.

She remembered the airplane being diverted and detained. The last thing she could recall was trying to resist a woman from giving her a shot. Everything after that was blank. She didn't know how long she had been there.

While contemplating her situation, a woman wearing a burka entered the room with a bowl of food and a bottle of water. She left the food on the floor and started to leave. "Wait, please, talk to me. I speak Arabic." The women ignored her.

The next day, a man entered the room. "How are you?" he asked as if they were friends.

"Why are you holding me?" she demanded.

He hit her in the face with his fists, making her lip bleed, and spit on her. She reeled from the blow. "When I ask you a question, answer me as becomes my position. Address me as Master Aklam. I own you. If you did not have some value to me, I would rape you and have you stoned to death.

"And regardless of the situation, I will have you before you leave. You now have something to look forward to because I am a great lover," he said.

After he left, she curled up in the fetal position in the corner of the room, dazed and struggling not to fall apart.

A week passed. She could feel reality fading away. She was beginning to think she wouldn't survive her ordeal when her captors decided to move her to a new location out of fear of keeping her in one place too long and being found by special forces they knew would be looking for her.

Two guards were walking her to a vehicle when Aklam, who had hit her, ordered the guards to bring her to his private quarters. She resisted, but the guards forced her into the building.

"I know you have been dreaming about having sex with me, so I am going to satisfy your desire," he bragged.

She noticed a rifle with a bayonet attached to the barrel lying on a table. The rifle was lying with the barrel pointing away from her. She would have to turn around, pick the weapon up, turn back around, and shoot or stab him before he could take the rifle from her.

"I see you admiring my rifle. Would you like to shoot me or stab me with the bayonet? Lovers don't do that," he said. "I want this encounter to elicit extreme emotion and pain. And just having sex with you would be without any passion. I want you to remember me for the rest of your life, so we will play a game. The rifle is loaded and ready to fire. All you have to do is turn around, pick it up, turn back around, and shoot or stab me before I take it from you. I can't think of any foreplay that would be more stimulating."

He backed up to the opposite wall about twelve feet from her, "I am already aroused, start the game whenever you are ready."

They both knew there was no way she could beat him at his game.

Her mind was racing when she recalled watching the women practice throwing rifles with bayonets attached to each other at the special operator training camp she had attended.

what the hell

nothing to lose

She backed up to the butt of the rifle and grasped the nylon shoulder strap where it attached to the butt of the stock with her right hand. She calmly looked at Aklam. "Master Aklam, may I say a few words before we make love?" she asked.

With the unexpected question and resultant mental lapse that relaxed his reflexes for half a second, she hurled the rifle by the sling with all her strength, spinning the rifle on a horizontal plane toward him. The rifle made half a revolution in the air, and like a spear, the bayonet penetrated his chest before he could react with even one step toward her.

With disbelief and a shocked look on his face, he collapsed to the floor.

She couldn't believe what had happened. The odds of this last-ditch tactic being successful were less than zero. She froze from the adrenalin rush for a minute before regaining her composure.

She figured no one would check on the guy for some time, fearing his anger for interrupting his having sex with her.

She found a backpack, grabbed bottles of water, US-made MREs, and a blanket.

She pulled the rifle, with the bayonet attached, from his chest. She wiped the blood off the bayonet onto his white shirt. Then, looking into his dying eyes, she kissed him on the cheek. "My darling Master Aklam, it is with great pleasure to watch the vile bastard you are drown in your own blood," she said with a smile.

She slipped from a rear window into an alley, climbed the compound wall, and escaped into the mountains.

She walked steadily until she found a place in the rocky terrain out of sight from any direction and tried to relax and figure out where she was. After unloading her gear, she climbed through the rocky hillside to a point where she could see the horizon in every direction.

She hoped to see the glow of a city, but there was nothing. Contemplating her options, she noticed the flashing navigation lights of an airplane moving across the night sky. Watching intently for thirty minutes, she observed several airplanes flying in the same direction.

Utilizing survival skill training from her operator courses, she determined the direction of north by observing the Big Dipper constellation of stars. With north established, she determined the airplanes were flying west toward the Mediterranean Sea.

Returning to the place she had chosen to camp for the night, she was removing items from her backpack when she realized she didn't have anything to start a fire. Even with the blanket she brought, it would be a cold, miserable night without a fire.

Wrapped in the blanket and eating an MRE, she again recalled survival school and the class on making a fire.

Foraging through the surrounding area, she gathered an armload of firewood. From what she had gathered, she made a tool from a straight piece of limb about sixteen inches long and a half inch in diameter. She also scraped two handfuls of dry shavings from another branch with the bayonet. She assembled the larger pieces of wood into a pile, ready to light on fire.

She took a bullet from the rifle's magazine and removed the projectile from the case that held the powder. She found a large rock with a bowl-type depression that would hold the gunpowder. She placed a handful of wood shavings on top of the gunpowder and pressed the end of the stick into the bowl. With the stick held vertically between the palms of her hands, she vigorously rotated it back and forth, causing friction to create enough heat to ignite the gunpowder, which in turn lit the shavings on fire. Then she gently placed more wood shavings on top of the burning powder, creating a small fire that she then transferred to the main pile, creating a larger fire.

Early the following day, after a meal, she started walking in a westerly direction. Again, using her survival training, she knew she should keep the sun to her back in the morning and in front of her in the afternoon to keep a westward heading. She had made a walking stick out of a sturdy tree limb that helped her negotiate the rugged terrain and also helped her stay on course by monitoring the sticks' shadow when held straight up and down.

On day three, she heard dogs barking in the distance behind her. They were trailing her.

She entered a canyon with a small stream running through it. Hoping to cut off her scent trail, she walked in the stream until her feet became numb from the icy water. She left the stream and took an animal trail up the canyon wall.

Reaching the top of the canyon wall to a plateau, she set up camp for the night. She feared being seen or the dogs scenting her, so she didn't build a fire.

It was a few minutes before dawn, and she was shivering uncontrollably. She packed up without eating and started walking to generate some body heat.

She had been walking for an hour or more when she stopped to eat an MRE and drink a bottle of water.

She heard the dogs again. She tried to pick up her pace, but her energy level was deteriorating. She came across another stream and walked in it until she couldn't feel her feet. She stumbled and fell to her knees in the freezing water. Struggling out of the water, she collapsed on the bank. She removed her shoes and socks and dried her feet with the blanket. With enough feeling back in her feet, she returned to the stream to retrieve the rifle she had dropped when she fell.

She found a sunny spot to rest and hung her clothing and shoes on a tree branch to dry.

She was drinking a bottle of water when she noticed the magazine that held the bullets was missing from the rifle's magazine well. She must not have properly seated the magazine in the mag well, and it fell out while she was walking or when she dropped the rifle in the water. She again waded into the stream looking for the magazine but could not find it.

Now the rifle was useless, and she didn't have gunpowder to build a fire.

She detached the bayonet from the rifle and threw the rifle into the deepest part of the stream where it couldn't be seen, or the dogs scent it.

The stream ran against a vertical cliff on one side and a tree line stretching a hundred yards wide on the other side before it met the desert.

She found two large trees that had fallen parallel to each other about six feet apart. She cut leafy branches and bushes to lay across the two trunks for protection from a light rain that had started. She gathered armloads of dry leaves to make a bed and insulate her body from the frigid air. She lay down and curled up under her blanket. In the quiet, she could hear gunfire in the distance but was too exhausted to react. Trembling from the cold, she drifted off to sleep exhausted and resigned to her fate.

Asleep for less than an hour, she was awakened by something shuffling in the leaves and then a blinding light in her face. Hopeless, yet defiant to the end, she held the bayonet out to the light, expecting a bullet to end her life in the next second.

"Ma'am, Sergeant Hunter Daniels, 75th Rangers, at your service."

The voice of an American soldier was bewildering. With the light out of her face, she saw three American soldiers standing over her.

One second, she was waiting for a bullet to end her life. The next was euphoria.

She took a hand that made her heart melt with the warmth of someone who cared about her and risked their life to rescue her.

They led her to a location where a helicopter could land.

She was wearing a waterproof jacket one of the soldiers had given her. She was drinking coffee and talking with the guys while waiting for a helicopter to pick them up.

It was raining hard now, but she didn't care. She was warmer now than she had been for over a month and safe.

I would walk through hell with these guys

CHAPTER XL

renewed spirit

Taylor was waiting for the helicopter rotor blades to stop. He approached it with a large umbrella as the door slid open. Kathryn exited the helicopter and walked to him under the umbrella. She took his free hand and gave him a humble kiss. "Is there someplace around here where a gal could get a drink and a good massage?"

After a lot of shampoo and soap, she let the warm water from the shower rain on her head and run down her body for a good ten minutes.

Wearing a white robe, she joined Taylor in the living room of his apartment.

He handed her a glass of wine. "I know there is a lot to talk about, but right now, I just want to lay in bed and listen to some soothing music while you rub my aching back? I promise I will return the favor."

It was mid-morning when Kathryn woke to the smell of coffee. Taylor was standing at the end of the bed, looking at the bruises and scratches on her, fantasizing about confronting the individuals who had done those things to her.

"Did I die last night? Am I in heaven?" she asked as she leaned back against her pillow and took the cup of coffee he offered.

He was eager to hear the account of her ordeal, but he knew she would have a debriefing sometime that afternoon, and it would be better to wait until after that.

They had breakfast on the veranda before she left for her hotel to get ready for her meeting.

Back in his apartment after the briefing, she was feeling strange. Her impulse was to turn the lights off, get in bed, and pull the cover over her head.

Taylor knew that was not what she needed, "That sounds good, but let's go for a walk first." She resisted at first but then agreed. As they walked, Taylor steered the conversation to lighthearted subjects. He tried to be funny and was, by being a total failure at the attempt. "Okay, I'm not Seinfeld."

A taxi took them to a bar on the beach. They had drinks and walked in the surf.

Returning to the city, they went to a favorite restaurant. After dining, they went into the restaurant's lounge and listened to a great piano player. "Thank you for insisting I get out and enjoy the good things in life instead of isolating myself and dwelling on the bad," she said.

"I know you are even angrier now and more determined to kill Konjanko after this incident, but you know being motivated purely by anger will cause you to make mistakes that could get you or a colleague killed. You must return to that tactical mindset you are so good at. After the trauma you've experienced, you must get away for a while and clear your mind. Otherwise, I fear you will be unable to put this thing behind you, negatively affecting your work. PTSD is real. Approach this as if you have a serious infection. Take some time off, and rest. Listen to Doctor Lawton," he said with a chuckle. She begrudgingly agreed to take a few days off and flew to California to visit family and friends.

Taylor considered contacting Abdul and working on the Konjanko project while Kathryn was gone but decided that could impede their collaborative planning rather than help. Instead, he took advantage of the time Kathryn was gone to write and put a pile of notes into coherent prose. Writing was becoming part of his ethos. He found himself exploring any dialogue through the mental prism of writing.

Two weeks at her family home in California was the right thing to do. She intentionally turned her lifestyle upside down. She prepared dinner for her family several times, went surfing with friends, and generally tried to embrace the mindset of her youth.

On her return, Taylor could see the renewed spirit in her eyes. "We've been invited to a dock party this evening, but I'm okay with preparing dinner at my apartment or going to a restaurant. Your call," he offered.

"Let's go to a nice restaurant, then lounge on my deck, listen to some relaxing music, and drink scotch until you carry my comatose body to bed."

Kathryn took a few days to catch up on work and was updated on the latest developments regarding Konjanko. Taylor contacted Abdul and set up a meeting with Kathryn and him.

***

"Taylor and I have forged a bond of trust through difficult times. And I know you are an integral factor in our relationship, even though we have never met. I will help in any way to bring justice to your friend's death. One thing I'm sure I can do is to find this mercenary and gain an understanding of how he works and his relationship with Konjanko," Abdul said.

"I appreciate your offer to help. Through your collaboration with Taylor, I know you are adamant about not working directly with the US military, and you may need time to consider the parameters of our relationship. We must have a good understanding of those boundaries.

"A foremost concern for me is the gender issue. I hesitate to bring it into the equation, but our cultural differences must be addressed. You will work directly with me, so factor that into your deliberation. If you see me as anything other than a fellow warrior, it won't work," Kathryn said emphatically.

"Taylor has spoken of your spirit and commitment to your work. I will acknowledge that I was raised in a culture quite different from the Western world, but I pride myself on using my God-given logic to evaluate an ideological tenet and not adhere to some mechanical dogma. I remember, as a child, questioning why women were treated differently.

"And consequently, I have developed a more inclusive attitude toward women over time and perhaps have even accelerated my evolution with conversations about the subject with our friend Mr. Lawton.

"I will challenge you to accept me with that same spirit. I will collaborate with you under the same parameters as with Taylor. Let's go hunting," Abdul asserted.

A meeting with CIA officials was arranged, and a private contractor entity was chosen for the best relationship. The private contractor term in this situation was nothing more than a handshake and understanding at the agency's highest level. It was also understood that the agency would deny the relationship if anything went wrong.

Taylor called Ed and suggested the three of them go sailing, and he would update him on the operation plans.

"Sure, I'm on my boat now. I will get ready to sail."

Taylor and Kathryn helped with releasing the dock lines and getting under sail.

"I know it's early, but I could use a glass of wine," she said.

Kathryn told Ed about Matt's death.

"I got the impression he was a straight shooter when he came on the boat with you. I'm sorry to hear of his death. I know you were close friends."

After a few minutes of conversation and updating everyone on the project, Kathryn was eager to discuss her plan to kill the people responsible for Matt's death.

CHAPTER XLI

an arms dealer

She presented her plan to become an arms dealer. "The new Kathryn Montgomery is the daughter of a recently deceased arms dealer. He was a major player with worldwide connections, and I intend to continue the business.

And being an analyst, I am familiar with most US weapon systems and speak the terminology.

"But I need a couple of associates with similar knowledge. I don't suppose either of you gentlemen would know a couple of guys that would qualify for the positions?" she asked with a chuckle.

After discussing numerous options regarding the operation, they returned to the marina.

A dock party was underway when they returned to Ed's slip, and Kathryn decided this would be a good time for her to try on her new persona.

She took a taxi back to her hotel suite to dress for the occasion. This new role she was taking on would be a radical change for her.

She rarely used makeup, but now she must wear

much more. She changed the color of her naturally light brown hair to black and put on glasses. She replaced her modest wardrobe with an obviously expensive one with matching jewelry. She tried to brush up on her social etiquette. She looked in the mirror as she was leaving. "Hello, I don't think we've met."

Taylor and Ed had remained at the marina to help prepare for the event well underway when Kathryn arrived. Her dress was appropriate for the occasion, but the hair, makeup, glasses, and demeanor transformation were amazing for Taylor to see. She knew most of the people from previous events, but no one spoke to her as if they had ever met.

In jest, Taylor approached her. "Hello, I'm Taylor. You must be new to the dock. Did you sail in today?"

She leaned forward and whispered to him. "Hi, I'm Kat. I'm not a sailor. I'm a hooker looking for a sailor."

Kathryn's arms dealer credentials had been authenticated by a CIA-operated arms dealer company in business for years to monitor the worldwide arms dealer network. The CIA had built a dossier on Kathryn's pseudo-father and his business. And the data had been discreetly disseminated into the arms dealer network.

Abdul had been diligently working on the Konjanko-Russian mercenary connection. He informed Kathryn and Taylor that Konjanko would be in Damascus in three weeks. He had been invited to the mansion of a powerful Syrian politician who was a major arms dealer.

Kathryn contacted a CIA operative and informed her of the situation. Three days later, she received an invitation to the clique.

"Damn, those people are good," she remarked.

"I've been studying the weapons we're purported to specialize in. I have been out of the Army for twenty years. There will be weapons and systems that I'm not familiar with," Taylor conceded.

"I will bring you up to speed. We have three weeks," she replied.

***

"The politician business must be lucrative, another incredible mansion," she remarked as the taxi approached the event.

Entering the house, Taylor took on the persona of Kathryn's bodyguard and business associate.

He reminded himself to not stay by her side but maintain the distance of a trained bodyguard. He would join her only at her direction.

Kathryn was talking to Abdul and another person when Taylor brought her a drink she had requested. "Thank you, my darling," in her best southern Syrian. Taylor nodded to her and returned to his position. Looking over the room, he could identify several bodyguards by their demeanor.

Konjanko arrived with an entourage of bodyguards and women. It was an hour before he worked his way around the room to Kathryn's location. He acknowledged Abdul while grasping Kathryn's hand and kissing it.

"Abdul, my friend, please, introduce me to this

beautiful woman."

She held her breath, fearing he might recognize her from the event at his place. She gagged at the thought that the bastard touching her was responsible for Matt's death.

"Victor, this is Kathryn Montgomery, Kathryn, Victor Konjanko," Abdul answered.

"Kathryn, what brings you to Damascus," he asked. She repeated the story the CIA had created for her. She knew he would quickly verify her credentials through the arms dealer network.

After a few minutes of small talk, Kathryn excused herself to go to the ladies' room with the intention of not returning to Konjanko but to work the room introducing herself to other arms dealers.

When the conversation got technical, she was convincing with her knowledge of the weapons she purported to have for sale or could broker.

Watching every move Konjanko made, Taylor observed him following her from one group to another and inquiring about what she had said in conversation.

The evening progressed, and Konjanko approached Kathryn again.

"I inquired about your business from several sources and am satisfied with your credentials. I think we should talk privately about how we might collaborate on a venture that I am involved with that could be lucrative for both of us," he said.

"That sounds interesting," as she gestured for Taylor to join them.

"Victor, this is Taylor Marshall. He worked for my father for years and is an indispensable associate of the company," she said.

Neither offered to shake hands.

It was apparent Konjanko's immediate dislike for Taylor.

Weeks had passed when Kathryn received a call from Konjanko's secretary asking to set up a meeting to discuss the possibility of doing business together. They would meet on his yacht anchored in Cooks Bay on the north shore of Tripoli.

"I don't like the security issues with meeting on a boat anchored offshore. We will be totally defenseless unless we take a security detail with us. There is no way Konjanko would do this if the situation were reversed. He may be testing you to see how you will react to his proposition. Refusing to meet on his terms may gain you more credibility," Taylor noted.

She contacted Konjanko's secretary and told her she would meet with him only if the boat was docked in the Cooks Bay marina.

Hours later, she received a call agreeing to her request.

The boat captain was waiting for them at the top of the walkway. He welcomed them aboard and escorted them to an outside lounge at the stern of the boat, where Konjanko was waiting. He kissed Kathryn's hand and ignored Taylor.

"Rejecting my request to meet out in the bay tells me you are not so eager to do business with me that you would put yourself in a vulnerable position. I appreciate a cautious business partner."

"If you want to live long enough to enjoy the fruits of this business, being cautious is good for your health," she said.

"Before we discuss a possible business venture, I need to know what Mr. Marshall's job is with your business," he said as he looked contemptuously at Taylor.

"Taylor was my father's right-hand man and has years of experience in the business. Taylor will be with me at every meeting and advise me on business matters. He will not participate in our conversations, but you are free to engage him if you wish." she replied.

"Very well, we shall work together within those parameters. Now let's talk about a business proposition. "A client is interested in a rifle scope recently acquired from the battlefield. This scope automatically calculates the data required to make perfect long-range shots by even an untrained person. Are you aware of this scope?" Konjanko asked.

"Yes, I am familiar with the scope. It is a rigorously controlled item by the manufacturer and the US military," Kathryn said.

"Can you acquire this scope?" he asked.

"I will make some inquiries and get back to you," she answered. After an hour of discussing other possible business transactions, she and Taylor left the yacht. They took a taxi to the airport and flew back to Cyprus.

They went to her hotel suite to discuss the

Konjanko meeting. Taylor made drinks. "Are you familiar with this scope?" she asked as she handed Taylor a folder with the technical specifications of the scope.

"I have heard about it, but I thought the company went out of business," he replied.

"The company did go out of business, but a CIA front company bought it and retained the personnel to continue developing and manufacturing the scope at a secret facility. It is incredible what the latest version of this scope is capable of. I was briefed on the loss of the scope Konjanko is referring to.

It is inevitable that devices like this will fall into enemy hands at some point. Fortunately, the scope is designed to self-destruct when tampered with. So, the technology can't be reverse engineered, therefore driving the price up exponentially. I'm sure Konjanko knows this and can sell one of these scopes for $250,000," she said.

"How do we ensure the Russian mercenary that killed Matt gets involved in the transaction?" Taylor asked.

"Let's start by inquiring about the scopes in the dealer network and see what happens," she replied.

"In the meantime, I will contact Abdul to see if he has been able to find out anything about the Russian," Taylor said.

CHAPTER XLII

plan the sting

Taylor and Abdul met at the primitive campsite, where Abdul's bodyguards first picked him up and brought him to Abdul's cave. The same place where Abdul had picked him up after they killed Rahid.

"We should name this place," Taylor said.

"Camp Brandy," Abdul replied.

"I like it," Taylor responded.

"The Russian mercenary we're looking for lives in Astrakhan, Russia. His name is Anton Orlov. I will meet with him and offer to sell him the scopes. And being a subordinate of Konjanko, he will inform him of my proposal.

"When Konjanko hears of my offer to the Russians, he will contact me wanting in on the deal. And when Kathryn advises Konjanko of her position regarding me, he will play one against the other to secure the best deal," Abdul said.

Three weeks had passed when Kathryn contacted Konjanko to tell him she could supply the scopes.

They met on his boat. "You are a brave woman

coming on my boat without your bodyguard," he said.

"I know you are not about to blow millions of dollars doing something stupid. What is the axiom, business before pleasure? There will be plenty of time to develop our relationship after our transaction is complete," she promised.

"I like the sound of that." He offered her a drink, but she refused. "No thanks, I've got to stay on top of my game dealing with you," she said.

"Alright, tell me the terms of our transaction."

"I can supply fifty scopes. The price is $125,000 each. Another term of our transaction has to do with Abdul-Hadi. You are friends and have done business together, but I don't want him involved in any part of this transaction. He is trying to run me out of business."

"But I saw you talking with him at my house."

"I don't want Abdul to suspect I know what he is doing. I have been informed that he is trying to discredit my reputation. A contract we were working on fell out because he made a mistake. He is now trying to divert the blame to me. I will be successful in this business even if I have to step over a few bodies," she replied.

"You are ruthless. I'm intrigued. Give me a few days to consider your offer, and I will contact you with my decision," he said.

She left the yacht.

Konjanko contacted Abdul and inquired about his offer to sell the scopes to the Russian without mentioning his dealings with Kathryn. Abdul suggested that selling the scopes to the Russian would bolster his image as a powerful warlord, and he could use the money to fund his army. He was willing to pay Konjanko a fee for allowing the transaction, knowing the Russian would relinquish the scopes to Konjanko after the transaction was complete.

After he met with Abdul, Konjanko met Kathryn again on his yacht to finalize the sale details.

"It has come to my attention that Abdul is offering to sell this scope to another party," he said.

"If what you say is true, it confirms our relationship is over," Kathryn replied.

"I have a proposal. I will purchase half the scopes from you and let my associate buy the other half from Abdul. The scopes that my associate buys will come to me anyway. Abdul's interest and mine have diverged over the last few years. He has aligned himself with people who conflict with my business and interests. I have been tolerant, but going behind my back and dealing directly with the Russian is too much. I will have the Russian eliminate him after the scopes are received," Konjanko said.

"I have no issue with your proposal, except I want the money you recover from Abdul," Kathryn said.

"You are a shrewd negotiator. I will agree to the terms," he said.

Kathryn met Taylor and Ed on Ed's boat. She reviewed the details of her conversation, finalizing the scope deal with Konjanko.

"The priority now is to coordinate the killing of Konjanko and the Russian Orlov. The timing will be critical. "I will meet with Abdul and tell him Konjanko's plan to have Orlov kill him when they meet to complete the scope sale," Taylor said.

Every operation detail was thoroughly reviewed. It was time to execute.

CHAPTER XLIII

execute the sting

Kathryn and Taylor were directed through a metal detector before they boarded Konjanko's yacht. They joined him on the aft deck.

"Please help yourself to the food and bar. Quang is a mixologist extraordinaire. He will make any cocktail you request the best you've ever had," he bragged.

"I am looking forward to a glass of your best champagne to celebrate the conclusion of our business transaction," Kathryn replied.

Taylor requested two glasses of tonic water with twists of lime.

The sun was setting as the crew disconnected shore power and cast off the dock lines. The yacht eased away from the dock and passed through the bay inlet and into the sea.

"To recap our agreement, when the vessel carrying the scopes contacts us, Taylor will join your captain on the bridge. After that, the crew will go to their quarters until our transaction is complete.

"Once our boat is close enough, a dinghy will

bring the scopes to your vessel for inspection. After inspecting the scopes to your satisfaction, you are to transfer 6.25 million USD equivalent value of Bitcoin to an account I will enter into the exchange website. Once the transfer is verified, Taylor and I will board our boat and leave. At that time, your crew may return to their stations, and you can be on your way," Kathryn said.

"I don't like it, but I will consent to your plan," Konjanko growled.

Abdul had arranged with the Russian Orlov to complete their scope deal while Taylor and Kathryn completed theirs. It was agreed that each of them would bring two support people. Abdul would send Orlov directions to where they would meet via GPS coordinates at the last minute. This would ensure he wouldn't be ambushed by Orlov's men. He would coordinate his transaction with Taylor and Kathryn.

As the two vehicles approached each other at the designated place in the desert, Abdul knew that Orlov intended to kill him after the scope sale was completed.

Before Orlov's arrival, his soldiers had dug fox holes in the ground and placed brush over the holes, concealing the person inside. When Abdul positively identifies Orlov he will signal the men in the containers to kill Orlov and his men.

Abdul was leaning against the hood of his truck. His two bodyguards were on each side of him a few yards apart, making it difficult to shoot them separately.

An armored Humvee leaving a trail of dust stopped fifty yards from Abdul's vehicle. A minute or two after the dust had blown away, two of Orlov's men exited the vehicle and unloaded two duffel bags. They carried the bags to Abdul. They unzipped both bags and emptied bands of hundred-dollar bills onto a large tarp that Abdul's men had laid out on the ground. Abdul's men examined the contents of the bags to verify that the money was genuine and there were no tracking devices or explosives hidden in the bags. Satisfied with their search, Abdul's men unloaded wooden crates containing the scopes.

Orlov's men brought the containers to him for his inspection.

After satisfactorily inspecting the scopes, he turned to Abdul with a big smile and arms held out, gesturing to embrace Abdul.

"Abdul, my friend," said Orlov as he walked toward him.

Convinced that it was Orlov, Abdul signaled his men concealed in the containers by speaking his name, "Orlov!"

It was over in a few seconds. Orlov and his men were cut down by automatic weapons fire, including two more men hiding in the Humvee.

Abdul texted Taylor an encrypted message confirming his transaction was complete.

Taylor whispered to Kathryn that Abdul's part of the mission was complete.

The CIA craft with the other half of the scopes appeared on the horizon. Taylor joined the captain on the bridge, and the crew was directed to their sleeping quarters below deck.

The two vessels stopped a hundred yards from each other. Ed and a crew member lowered a powered dinghy into the water, loaded the scopes, and motored to Konjanko's boat. The scopes were unloaded for Konjankos inspection. He removed a scope from one of the containers and examined it by turning it on and looking through the lens. "I would like to see the scope in action, but the waves moving the boat around make that impossible. I will take your word that they work properly," Konjanko said.

"The scopes were tested and updated with the latest firmware to ensure your satisfaction. I want to build a good relationship with you and make a lot of money so I can buy a yacht like this one," as she said all the right things to put him at ease.

"I am ready to complete the transaction after you agree to dine with me this evening without your bodyguard," Konjanko said.

"That's not in the agreement, but I accept your request and look forward to that time," she smiled as she cringed inside at the thought.

Upon completion of the money transfer, Konjanko and Kathryn retired to the aft deck for a celebratory glass of champagne.

Handguns had been secretly passed to Taylor and Kathryn by Ed when he brought the scopes aboard Konjanko's boat.

Konjanko was unaware that Taylor had locked the captain and crew in their quarters at gunpoint.

With his back to her, he worked to remove the cork from a bottle of champagne. In the interim, Kathryn retrieved a 45-caliber automatic pistol from her undergarment.

After pouring two glasses of champagne, Konjanko turned to see Kathryn pointing a pistol at him.

"What is this," he asked, incredulous at the turn of events.

"This is for my friend Matt whom you had the Russian kill. It is the beginning of your last few minutes of life. Your comrade Orlov has already paid the price.

"I am going to take great pleasure in ending your criminal and evil life," Kathryn said in a stone-cold timbre.

"Hold on, I will pay you any amount of money you want. You will be wealthy. You would be foolish to kill me."

Gripping the pistol with both hands, she shot Konjanko multiple times in the chest, knocking him over the railing into the sea. Then she calmly picked up the bottle of champagne and took a couple of swallows before she threw it at Konjanko as his body drifted away from the boat. "Matt, my friend, rest in peace."

Taylor released the captain from his cabin and forced him to stand on the bow of his boat. He was threatened with being shot if he moved. Taylor and Ed loaded the scopes back into the dinghy, and with Kathryn, they motored to the waiting craft.

Konjanko's captain could see Ed holding a rifle at

the ready from the CIA boat. He was to stay there until he was contacted by marine radio and told when he could unlock his crew and go on their way.

Kathryn Ed and Taylor took the CIA boat's helicopter to Camp Brandy.

It was Kathryn's first trip to the camp. Abdul was there waiting for them.

"A better name for this place would be Camp Spartan," Kathryn joked as she observed the simple firepit and skeletons of a couple of lean-to sheds in the middle of the nowhere desert.

"Don't bad mouth Camp Brandy. Abdul and I are considering opening a destination BBQ joint and Monster Truck venue here when the war ends," Taylor said.

With a fire blazing under a full moon, Abdul filled their glasses with Brandy and opened a box of Italian cigars.

After offering the cigars to Taylor, he hesitated to offer one to Kathryn but held the box out to her. "I will have to brush my teeth, shower, and wash my hair if I smoke one of those things. But what the heck, this is a special occasion," she said and took one.

With glasses filled and cigars lit, Taylor offered a toast as he raised his glass, "To Kat Macallan. This was no easy day. You are one indomitable warrior."

CHAPTER XLIV

will this ever end

Taylor was reclining in a beach chair at a private bungalow accessible only by boat or helicopter on the Greek island of Rhodes.

He watched sandpipers dance in rhythm with the waves as they searched for food each time a wave retreated from the sand beach. The solitude was splendid for writing. With no distractions, he had made considerable progress.

He had been there for over a week and written for hours daily. On this day, after writing for several hours, he had lain back in his beach chair and pulled his Boonie hat over his eyes to rest a few minutes.

Just as he was drifting off to sleep, he heard the sound of a helicopter. Peering from under his hat, he watched the helicopter land on the beach. A woman exited the craft wearing a backpack. After the helicopter left, she gazed into the ocean for a few minutes before waving to Taylor. Then, walking to the water's edge, she changed into a bathing suit and dove into the surf. Taylor watched her for a few minutes before bringing a couple of beach towels and joining her in the surf. "After what we've been through with Konjanko, I desperately needed this. Thank you for finding this place. It is breathtaking," she sighed.

The sun was sinking into the ocean as he built a fire at the water's edge. He brought beach chairs and a cooler of wine and scotch. He bluetoothed a speaker to his cell phone and played her favorite music.

After sleeping until late morning, he made coffee from beans he had bought from a market near the airport when he arrived. The vendor said it was the best coffee on the planet. For breakfast, he prepared his famous (in his mind) pancakes made with orange juice.

"Oh, my goodness, these are the best pancakes. You must give me the recipe," she urged.

"You will have to persuade me with something special," he grinned.

"I can't imagine what that would be," she laughed.

"You're a smart gal. I'm confident you will figure it out."

They made the best of every day: sailing, snorkeling, hiking, and looking for buried treasure. They rented a sailboat and sailed through the countless Greek islands.

It was late in the day, and they were looking for a protected cove or bay to anchor for the night when they noticed three sailboats anchored in a small bay. They furled the sails and motor into the bay. They motored close enough to speak to the people on one of the boats. A tanned, gray-haired woman approached the railing of her boat.

"Ahoy, mate, we're sailing in unfamiliar waters. Is this a good place to anchor for the night," Taylor asked.

"Yes, it is a great place. It is shallow enough that anchoring is easy, and being leeward of the island helps keep the water calm.

"After you've anchored, come join us and our friends for happy hour," she said, pointing to another boat anchored a few yards away.

Taylor and Kathryn set the anchors and squared away the boat for the night.

They were lowering the dinghy into the water to visit their new friends when Kathryn received a message from a colleague. She grimaced as she looked up from her laptop. "Abdul has been taken prisoner by a rogue warlord. He was lured to a fake meeting to improve relations with several other warlords."

"Damn, will this ever end?" Taylor cursed. "It will take three days of hard sailing to return to Crete, but we must return to Erbil as soon as possible. See if you can get a helicopter here in the morning to pick us up. I will arrange for the rental company to send someone to sail the boat back to Crete," Taylor said.

"There is nothing more we can do at this time. Let's have a drink with these folks and explain that a business issue has come up that requires our attention," she replied.

After a pleasant visit and explaining that an emergency had come up, they returned to their sailboat. They packed their bags in preparation for leaving the following day.

Taylor had arranged with their new friends to pick them up from their boat and dinghy them to the beach.

They were waiting when the helicopter landed. They boarded the craft and headed back to Crete to pick up the rest of their luggage before continuing to the airport, where a jet was waiting to take them to Erbil.

CHAPTER XLV

rescue Abdul

Taylor and Kathryn met with a CIA operative. "At this time, there is no information regarding Abdul's location or any demands from his captors," the operative advised.

"I should go to Abdul's new headquarters compound and contact his bodyguards. If anyone knows what is going on, it would be them," Taylor said.

"You don't know what the situation is at his camp. You may be shot on sight. Go to Camp Brandy instead. His bodyguards know that Abdul meets you there under such circumstances.

"It's a long shot but try that first. It will only take a couple of days at the most." Kathryn said.

It was 03:00 when the helicopter dropped Taylor off a mile from the camp. He used his night vision goggles to scan the area for any activity. It was an hour before sunrise, so he tried to relax by lying down with his head on his backpack and gazing at the stars.

At first light, Taylor could see the camp was

deserted. The only activity was a herd of wild camels making their way through the valley. The plan was for Taylor to stay until midnight. If no one showed up the helicopter would return and pick him up.

Hours passed, and the heat intensified. He stretched a camouflaged tarp between two large boulders to block the sun. It was difficult to keep alert. Time had slowed to a crawl.

For the hundredth time, he scanned the distance with his binoculars. This time he spotted a faint cloud of dust. Watching the cloud intently as it grew larger, the familiar white Mercedes appeared. The vehicle stopped at the camp, and Abdul's bodyguards got out. They stood in front of their vehicle a few minutes before walking to a crudely built picnic-style table in the shade of a gnarled, half-dead tree. They sat down and smoked cigarettes. They acted as if they were waiting for someone.

Taylor had his bulletproof vest on and his rifle at the ready. He had tied a white T-shirt to a long stick he had found and waved it above his head to get their attention.

They stood and waved, acknowledging him. As he walked toward them, he looked for any movement from their vehicle that could conceal someone. When he reached the vehicle, he opened the door with the barrel of his rifle, ready to shoot if necessary. Satisfied with his search, he relaxed and told them he was happy to see them as he handed them a carton of American cigarettes. He asked them to tell him everything they knew about Abdul's imprisonment.

They told him An Al-Radea-backed warlord had been trying to take over Abdul's province ever since Abdul killed Rahid and consolidated the two provinces under his control.

He was being held in a small village in the mountains near the Turkish border. The warlord demanded that Abdul's second-in-command meet with him at a designated place in the mountains with twenty of Abdul's soldiers. At the meeting, Abdul must tell his men that he will disband his army and leave Iraq. The twenty soldiers will be killed if he doesn't leave Iraq. After it was verified that Abdul had left the country, his soldiers would undergo a reeducation program to ensure their loyalty to the new warlord.

Regardless of what happened, the bodyguards felt there was no way to save Abdul or his army.

"We're not going to let that happen, I promise you," Taylor said.

Taylor had a map of Iraq. He asked the bodyguards to narrow the search area for Abdul the best they could. Once they agreed on the general area, Taylor linked up with a drone in that zone. He turned its camera on to display the terrain. He asked the bodyguards to look at the display on his laptop. After a few minutes of studying the map, they pointed to a village. Taylor zoomed in on the village. They agreed that was where Abdul was being held.

He contacted Kathryn via satellite phone and gave her the details of the situation.

"This is a tough one. The warlord is holding all the

cards," she replied.

"I'm thinking we should play his game, abduct or kill the bastard," Taylor growled.

"Well, that's pretty straightforward and may be the best action to take," she said.

Taylor directed the bodyguards to go to their camp, muster the men the warlord had demanded, and bring them to Camp Brandy.

While Taylor was waiting for the men, he contacted Kathryn and requested a Chinook helicopter. It was capable of carrying all of the troops at one time.

It took thirty-six hours for the bodyguards to return with the soldiers.

The helicopter transported Taylor and the soldiers to a location about two miles from the warlord's compound, so they wouldn't be detected.

The deadline for the meeting demanded by the warlord was two days away. The warlord and his soldiers were relaxing. Some played a card game while others played soccer inside the walled compound.

One of the warlords' men yelled and pointed to the sky. A drone controller was directing a remote-controlled civilian-type airplane to land where the warlord would see it. A fire had been activated on the airplane to make it look distressed before landing a few hundred yards from the village.

The warlord took the bait and got into a vehicle. He ordered his men to load up in their trucks and follow him while leaving a few men to guard the camp. They rushed out of the compound, heading to the plane.

Taylor and the twenty armed soldiers that would be traded for Abdul hid in the brush and trees growing against the back wall of the compound.

They breached the wall, and the soldiers who didn't go to the crash site were killed or taken prisoner.

They forced an enemy soldier to take them to Abdul, where he was released from a locked room. Overcome with joy to see Taylor and his men, he could hardly speak. "I don't know what to say," Abdul said.

"We'll have a good conversation soon enough," Taylor said.

Like most walled villages in Iraq, there was a guard tower on one corner of the compound. Taylor and Abdul climbed into the tower. Taylor handed Abdul a sniper rifle, "You should have the privilege of putting a bullet in this bastard.

The warlord and his soldiers were unaware of what was happening.

Abdul was looking through the rifle scope, and Taylor was looking through his binoculars. They scanned the soldiers milling around the airplane, looking for the warlord.

"Most of the time, the soldiers wear a white head wrap, and the commanding officer will wear a black headband so he can easily be seen by his men when in combat," Abdul said.

"It also makes him a bulls-eye target," Taylor said.

After scanning the crash site for a few minutes, Abdul spotted the warlord.

"I see him. Look to the right of the airplane a few yards. I see his face. That's him for sure."

"I've never seen the guy. If you're sure that's him, take him out," Taylor replied.

The crack of the weapon firing echoed across the valley as the bullet slammed into the warlord's chest. His men were stunned when they saw him lying in a pool of blood.

When the warlord's men looked toward the compound from where the sound of the shot came, they saw Abdul's men lining the compound's walls. The battle flag of Abdul's army was flying from the guard tower flagpole.

The warlord's soldiers were out in the open with nowhere to hide. They lined up in a single row and dropped to their knees. They locked their fingers together on top of their heads and surrendered.

CHAPTER LXVI

celebrating Abduls' rescue

Abdul's camp was busy preparing to celebrate their victory over the rival warlord and the inclusion of his territory under Abdul's control.

After celebrating with his people throughout the day, he headed for Camp Brandy. He instructed his driver to let him out at the camp, drive a distance away, and wait for him to signal when he wanted them to return.

Taylor had built a fire and was waiting for him.

Abdul handed him a bottle. "Here is that 30-year-old scotch you've wanted for so long. But about the 30-year-old maiden, I think you've got that covered with the namesake of this scotch."

Taylor took the bottle from Abdul, "30-year-old Macallan. Man, I've wanted to try this forever."

Abdul poured them each a couple of fingers and held his glass out to Taylor. "I was a derisive ass when we first met, and later it was friendly banter, but I can no longer bring myself to refer to you as "Infidel." You have twice saved my life. There are no words to express my gratitude. I will simply salute you as my brother," he said, raising his glass to Taylor.

"I believe the ass-saving score is even. The journey to the relationship we have developed through the throws of war has been extraordinary. Living on life's edge tends to forge enduring bonds of brotherhood, salute," Taylor said as they touched glasses.

"Also, recalling the conversation we had when we first met regarding my assessment of the Iraqi culture that led to your threat of shooting me in the head and leaving me in the desert for the vultures to eat has changed. Civilian and soldier have enlightened me regarding your culture in the most positive way. Experiencing the daily lives of the Iraqi people in real time has made me think more purposefully. I have gained an insight that can be acquired only through personal interaction," Taylor asserted.

They continued to talk and recall those times of struggle and those of satisfaction for another hour, putting off that time they would go their separate ways.

After a long handshake and heartfelt embrace, Taylor watched the Mercedes disappear into the desert.

CHAPTER LXVII

déjà vu

Taylor was on Hayman Island, part of Australia's Great Barrier Reef. He was reclining in a beach chair at a private bungalow accessible only by boat or helicopter. He was watching pelicans dive for fish and a colony of seagulls screeching at one another over a bit of food.

Writing with no distractions, he had made modest progress. He had been alone for over two weeks and had written for hours every day. He retrieved a beer from his cooler before laying his laptop on it. He sipped the beer as he mulled over several past events that he thought should be added to his manuscript. After a few minutes, he lay back in his beach chair and pulled his Boonie hat over his eyes.

Just as he was drifting off for a nap, he heard the sound of a helicopter. Using the bottle of beer to push the brim of his hat up enough to peer from underneath it, he watched it approach and land on the beach. A side door opened, and a woman with a backpack slung over one shoulder exited the aircraft.

The helicopter lifted off, leaving her on the beach. With hands on her hips, she gazed into the ocean. After a moment, she turned and waved to Taylor before she began stripping down to her underwear. She threw each piece into the air as she walked to the water.

He watched her play in the surf before meeting her at the water's edge and offered her a cocktail, "Lemon Myrtle?"

"You remembered."

"You're not one to forget," he said with a chuckle.

He tossed her bag into a dinghy he had pulled up on the beach. They motored out to a sailboat anchored a few yards off the beach.

Weighing anchor and heading into the wind, Taylor hoisted the mainsail, and with a fair wind off the starboard bow ...